# SPECIAL MESSAGE TO READERS

## THE ULVERSCROFT FOUNDATION
### (registered UK charity number 264873)

was established in 1972 to provide funds for research, diagnosis and treatment of eye diseases. Examples of major projects funded by the Ulverscroft Foundation are:-

- The Children's Eye Unit at Moorfields Eye Hospital, London
- The Ulverscroft Children's Eye Unit at Great Ormond Street Hospital for Sick Children
- Funding research into eye diseases and treatment at the Department of Ophthalmology, University of Leicester
- The Ulverscroft Vision Research Group, Institute of Child Health
- Twin operating theatres at the Western Ophthalmic Hospital, London
- The Chair of Ophthalmology at the Royal Australian College of Ophthalmologists

You can help further the work of the Foundation by making a donation or leaving a legacy. Every contribution is gratefully received. If you would like to help support the Foundation or require further information, please contact:

## THE ULVERSCROFT FOUNDATION
### The Green, Bradgate Road, Anstey
### Leicester LE7 7FU, England
### Tel: (0116) 236 4325

### website: www.foundation.ulverscroft.com

Jeremy Cameron spent several years working in hostels for the homeless and twenty years living and working in Walthamstow. During this period he wrote a series of novels set in the area, featuring Nicky Burkett.

You can discover more about the author at www.jeremycameron.co.uk

# IT WAS AN ACCIDENT

After four years of incarceration, Nicky Burkett is released onto the sunny streets of North London's most edgy area: Walthamstow. The guy wants to go straight. The beautiful Noreen Hurlock wants him to go straight — in fact, she vows she won't come near him if he doesn't. So he tries. But events and people conspire against him. The 'work' he is offered proves dodgy. He is attacked. His mates are attacked. Even running to Jamaica isn't enough to keep him out of trouble. The time has come for the fight back to begin . . .

*Books by Jeremy Cameron*
*Published by Ulverscroft:*

VINNIE GOT BLOWN AWAY

# JEREMY CAMERON

◆

# IT WAS AN ACCIDENT

*Complete and Unabridged*

# ULVERSCROFT
*Leicester*

First published in Great Britain in 1996

First Large Print Edition
published 2016
by arrangement with
HopeRoad Publishing Ltd
London

The moral right of the author has been asserted

Copyright © 1996 by Jeremy Cameron
All rights reserved

A catalogue record for this book is available
from the British Library.

ISBN 978–1–4448–2972–3

Published by
F. A. Thorpe (Publishing)
Anstey, Leicestershire

Set by Words & Graphics Ltd.
Anstey, Leicestershire
Printed and bound in Great Britain by
T. J. International Ltd., Padstow, Cornwall

This book is printed on acid-free paper

# 1

Time used to be you got out of nick eight o'clock went round the corner got a bit of breakfast.

These days more likely you got out half past nine fifty miles out of town some gaff up Sheppey middle of winter. Some bird picked you up you got lucky.

Me I got out Wandsworth middle of the morning not a café in sight. Cross the street wait half an hour on a bus up Tooting. Strange no Roller sitting there no TV camera not even the *Walthamstow Guardian*.

Down Tooting they never even sold the *Guardian*. Got a *Mirror*. I already passed my gear out on visits only got a bag. Jacket went out of style three years ago, haircut was Vidal Convict. Looked a right tosser me, reckoned everyone on the fucking tube clocked me.

Got the tube out of Tooting Bee up Euston. Got lost there, geezers giving it shove everywhere. You shoved a geezer in nick meant plenty agg, you got one over the bonce in the recess. Round Euston though it seemed you took no notice.

I got the Victoria up the front. Twenty

minutes later Walthamstow Central.

I went up the stairs, escalator still not working. No ticket collector, one bleeding time I got a ticket I never needed it. Out in the rain. Went 'All right' to Terri worked the flowers. Clocked around the skyline, never recognised half of it. Buildings gone, buildings come. Boozer was still there over the road though so reckoned to get a fucking pint of lager.

Jesus they doubled the damage.

Got the pint anyway, went and sat down the corner for a think. It was eleven o'clock. Reckoned I got to go up Mum's, get round Kelly's see Danny the kid, maybe put it up Kelly celebrate getting out, see a few mates. Make myself busy. Felt like it get round Grosvenor Park Rd and sign on, give them the green form and order some dosh. Took about a year so start right off.

I sipped the lager and beadied round the punters. Never knew no geezer. They still clocked me funny. Never fancied that boozer anyway except Friday nights it was always good for a rucking.

Then would you believe it a heavy mitt came down my shoulder. Jesus I near as hit the ceiling and shit myself the same time. Nicked already and I only came out two hours!

'Morning Nicky.'

'Fuckin' Nora what'd I do?'

'Nothing Nicky you ain't done nothing. Just a chat. Buy you a half?'

'Ain't that just typical you fucking geezers George? Been away four fucking years and you buy me a half!'

'Glass is almost full Nicky.'

'Won't be I empty it.'

'All right I'll buy you a pint when you empty it. Mind if I sit down?'

He sat down. First person let on to me after doing my time had to be George my warrant officer. Fucking couldn't owe any fines yet surely.

'How you feeling Nicky?'

'Fucking great. Get out done my bird, come out the Central don't recognise nowhere don't know no-one, go down the boozer quiet pint of lager first geezer clocks on to me got to be a fucking pig. Fucking great.'

'Don't be like that Nicky.'

'Knew the time I got here or what George?'

'Got a fair idea. Rang the nick this morning. They told me you got a travel warrant up Walthamstow. Then they told me the time you got out.'

'Ain't you got no villains to feel George, no-one not paid their parking fines you got to beat up in the cells? Didn't you ought to be throwing them in the wagon up court this time of day?' George always hit you on the warrants first off like seven in the morning. Reckoned he always came that time knew he got a cup of tea. Sometimes stayed on a bit of breakfast. One time he paid one of my fines on the hush, knew I was a kid got no dosh, felt sorry for me.

'On holiday a couple of days Nicky.'

'Funny fucking holidays spend it hanging round Walthamstow Central. They closed down Tenerife?'

'Wanted to see you Nicky. You got a moment?'

'Fuck all else.'

'Wanted to get a chat with you Nicky. They reckoned I was the best person to approach you like.'

'I got it. I owes you 50p still outstanding my last fine.'

'Nothing like that Nicky. All your fines got cleared up years ago son. We lodged them like when you went away. No I've got a sort of a proposal for you Nicky.'

'Bit of business? Piece of work? Want me retail the gear they got up Chingford nick? Bit of blow, few electricals? Leave it out George I mean do me a favour.'

'Nothing like that Nicky. You know I'm

only a warrant anyway. And I'll thank you not to talk about my Chingford colleagues like that.'

Nearly made me throw up my lager.

'Nicky there's some people in the force who reckoned you might be able to help them with a proposal.'

'Fucking roll on George I reckon I might be brassick only I ain't a fucking grass yet. Anyway I thought they done away with the Regionals and their big dosh years past?'

'Nicky you got to understand. I'm just here to help out like an intermediary. You know me I never get involved in all that stuff. Matter of fact,' he stared in his beer, 'I never even wanted to get involved this far. You and me we go way back, eh Nicky? You were always straight with me, I was straight with you.'

'True enough George.' Arrested me fifteen times still expected his cup of tea. When our Sharon got her kid and no dosh there was George brought a pram round reckoned his family never wanted it any more.

'Only I said I'd talk to you, make the introductions if you wanted.'

'Sort of a fence like. This don't hardly seem to get no better George.'

He cleared his throat just going to think up his affidavit and that. Only then there was a major interruption. Just the most beautiful bit

5

of tit in Walthamstow was all, walked in the door like it was the palace.

'Fucking Noreen!' I went.

'Hello Nicky, all right?' she went.

'Fucking roll on Noreen what you doing here?'

'That's not a very nice reception now Nicky is it?' Only she was cackling. Only fucking Noreen Hurlock, Ricky Hurlock's big sister worked up British Airways, smartest bit of tart you ever clocked. Bleeding beautiful. Then she probably got a geezer and eight kids since I went away. Funny I never asked about her on visits. Never wanted to hear I reckon.

'You got a geezer and eight kids since I went away Noreen or you still available?'

She cackled again. 'Don't change do you Nicky? I've been sent here like a messenger, find you and take you somewhere.'

'Jesus there's two messengers now. Meet George my warrant.'

'Hello Mr Marshall all right?' she went. Never got him professional George she was straight as a ruler that Noreen and all her family, probably knew him up the badminton club or some shit.

'Hello Noreen luv all right?'

'I got to take you somewhere. There's people waiting to show you something Nicky.'

'Jesus I reckoned they all forgot me now I got out. Have to get round Mum's Noreen say all right.'

'Then there's your Danny with Kelly.'

'You got to remind me.' Whenever I tried to get on the subject of Noreen and me like having a bit, then she always had to mention the case of me being a daddy. Seemed to reckon there was a connection. She looked a bit older now Noreen only fuck me still got the same shape, not sagging anywhere.

'You sure you ain't got no kiddies while I been away Noreen? Ain't you working today you got the elbow?'

She cackled. 'Matter of fact I got promoted Nicky only I took a day off today see you get out.'

'Jesus you never gave me half a piece of boiled yam before Noreen. You ain't got prison fever I suppose?' Birds all over London went leery over cons, fuck knows why, lasted about as long as a quick handjob and the first giro.

'Scuse me,' went George. 'Scuse me you two lovebirds. Just before you go off together over the marshes, d'you reckon you could give us two minutes, Noreen, me and Nicky here? Two minutes is all?'

'Course Mr Marshall no problem.' She went out the road followed by half the

7

customers all wanted to buy her a rum and coke.

Only now I was pissed. Pint and a half lager I was anybody's, had to make do with blow all the time in the nick. Touch that hooch in there and you're gone, send you blind and talk like a Geordie.

'Now then Nicky,' goes George.

'Now then George.'

'Lads got a proposition to put to you.'

'Want to make me chief inspector? Give me the story on them drugs keep disappearing out of property or my watch went missing up Chingford? Have a whip round so I don't need no loan off the Social?'

'Last one's a bit close Nicky.'

'Eh?'

'Like I'm only a messenger you know.'

'Fucking wind it up George I'm getting GBH of the earhole here.'

'Well like the lads reckon you might be in a position to help them Nicky.'

'Help fucking Old Bill? Help them over a cliff.'

'Now then Nicky I'm Old Bill too you know.'

'Yeah only you ain't Chingford CID. Fucking DS Grant eh, them's geezers always want an assist only they generally got a boot under your hooter when they want it.'

'Funny you should mention DS Grant Nicky. You not heard?'

'Heard what?'

'News must be slow these days. DS Grant got murdered last Saturday night.'

'Jesus.'

'Got shot. Up by the forest.'

'Maybe they reckoned he was a deer. Weren't leaping over no fences at the time?'

'He was investigating.'

'Investigating some backhander I reckon. Jesus, DS Grant got plugged. Calls for a celebration George want another?'

'Nicky you know DS Grant was my colleague.'

'Kiss my arse George you love him like I love him.'

'Yes but you can't have people going round shooting police officers Nicky you know that, ain't right.'

'Beats mugging old ladies.'

'So the lads knew you were coming out, knew DS Grant put you the way of sorting your last little matter. Knew you handled it. Lads put your name up. Reckoned you might like to put the ears out. Lads aren't getting a lot of news coming in up to now.'

'And a few sobs in it eh?'

'Lads had a whip like I said.'

'Had a fucking whip? So it ain't official?

9

Jesus. First day out and I got ninety homeless discharge, half of it gone on a pint of lager, you and your mates reckon dosh me a pony and I bound to put the squeal on some geezer plugged a copper and fucking DS Grant at that. You got to be a sandwich short of a picnic, George.'

'One other thing Nicky.'

'Eh?'

'They got your mate in the bargain.'

'What mate?'

'Your mate Rameez.'

Had to cackle.

'You reckon Rameez my mate George? You marked Rameez my mate?'

'You did the piece of work together on that last business.'

You had to laugh eh. Pigs reckoned they were smart. Got the wrong grasses maybe. Business it was, strictly business Rameez and me.

'They near as put his eye out.'

'You makin' joke George? Put his eye out?'

'And took off a finger. He's up Whipps Cross.'

'Didn't reckon he was up clubbing. He got protection?'

'Twenty-four hour. Only he ain't talking.'

'Sure they never took his tongue out in the bargain?'

We clocked our beer. That Noreen still waiting by the machine.

'Just wondered if you were interested Nicky. There's feelings running very high when a copper gets killed. Lot of people don't approve, even villains reckon it's out of order. Then again you put the questions on that last one, got the right noise, and I might say you were successful finding a solution too in the bargain.'

'Leave it out George. Manslaughter not murder you know that. Never planned nothing.'

'Yes of course Nicky. And people did say DS Grant slipped you the word on who was the main man.'

'Big fucking man DS Grant made himself busy.'

'And Rameez being your mate. And how that last business was after your mate Vinnie got blown away.'

'Rameez ain't no mate of mine George you got your whisper wrong.'

'Well that's as maybe. Only we thought, mention it now, give you the weekend to settle down then you might like to consider it. Fair bit of spending in it like I say. You only got to let me know if you're in the frame.'

'Fuck me George.'

'See you around Nicky.'

I sat there staring up the walls. No doubt what the real message was. Straight out of nick and Old Bill wanted me to go round plunging geezers.

Enough to make you lose faith in the British police eh.

'Noreen,' I went, 'I got to get some grub and that I'm pissed as a rat not used to this lager.'

'All right Nicky let's come on round the corner.'

So we went round the corner in the market and I got pattie and chips and coffee. Noreen had a diet coke, got to keep a watch on those tits of hers.

Got to be a doddle this release.

# 2

'So what's the story Noreen?' I went over my pattie.

'Can't say nothing now Nicky, like a secret.'

'Why they send you?'

She went confused, like blushed only she just went darker how black people do.

'They reckoned you'd come if I met you Nicky. Wouldn't think it was like a set-up or something.'

'You ain't changed your mind about a bit of nookie with me Noreen I suppose?'

'Piss off Nicky,' she laughed. Always tell that Noreen passed exams on account of how she went 'piss off', very polite. In the bargain she never put any nookie round my way, showed she passed her exams.

So there we were sitting in the gaff down the market getting my pattie. And I was supping my coffee and goggling her boobies. Then would you believe what happened but some geezer I never knew walked in came straight up. Big bald geezer about forty.

'You Nicky Burkett?' he went.

'No she is.'

'Got a bit of work put your way.' He plonked himself down our table. Big bald fat geezer. Belly coming out his jeans. Probably lived up Waltham Way.

'Do me a favour geezer I just got out the fucking nick. Spend the discharge first eh?' Hard to credit, there I was never knew what day it was, only wanted a pint of lager and put it up some bird and he was there offering up a bit of work.

'Plenty shekels in it.'

'Look feller I ain't clocked me mates yet, been round me mum's.'

'Plenty in it.'

'Like?'

'Five.'

'Five?'

'Big ones.'

Middle of the fucking eater, there he was talking five big ones.

'Spot of kiting? Stealing milk bottles?'

'Geezer rubbed out. Stepping on a man's toes. Give you the sub-contract.'

Then he wrote a number on a napkin, went out the door, Jesus.

Geezers kept wanting me to kill geezers. Been out half an hour. First George the warrant, never mention it himself and maybe even not want it, only the next pig up the line had to mention. Now this geezer. For five poxy grand. All on account of I had an accident one time.

Noreen was shitless couldn't believe her jam pies. 'Jesus Nicky,' she went.

Welcome to the zoo.'

'Jesus he wanted you to kill someone.'

'General idea.'

'How'd he mean sub-contract?'

'They hand him or his mates twenty, he gives me five. Take the rest for the introduction to the business.'

'Jesus Nicky.'

'You finished your coke?' Noreen was so straight she never even had a bent MOT. No-one came round theirs wanting them rub geezers out. She finished her coke.

Then I was out the door, forgot you had to pay. Never had to the last few years. Noreen doshed.

Then we crossed over Hoe St, missed all the traffic even though I was still pissed. Started up Church Hill past the dole. 'Reckon I ought to sign on Noreen?' I went. 'Get that out the way?'

'In a bit Nicky. We'll get that done this afternoon. Only first I want to take you up the road here.'

'Sounds good to me.' Except I was cream crackered could do with a good lie down. We walked up the hill past the sorting office

15

turned left on Howard Rd.

'What happen Noreen?'

'Just a minute Nicky you'll see. Be patient man. Fortunes weren't built in a day.'

'Weren't built in Walthamstow neither.' Anyone but Noreen I'd be spacy by now reckon it was a hit. Noreen was so pure it was painful. We trotted along past a few more doors then stopped. We went up a house and Noreen used a key.

'You shacked here now Noreen?'

'You'll see Nicky.'

Inside the door were two more doors, one the downstairs flat the other by the stairs for the other one. Noreen turned another key and we went upstairs. People were moving there. Someone went 'Put the drink out they're coming up.' Bit more reassuring that, on account of they don't put the drink out when they plan on slicing you.

'Yo Nicky!'

We turned the corner in the main room.

'YO NICKY!'

Jesus.

It was the collection. It was Sherry McAllister and Jimmy Foley and Ricky Hurlock and Dean Longmore and Wayne Sapsford and Paulette James and Julie Seagrave and Brendan Streeter and Elvis Littlejohn and Shelley Rosario and Javed Khan and Aftab Malik. It was the collection of my mates and then it was one or two I scrapped against. Half of them geezers you never trusted on taking your grannie home, have to steal a wheelie for it. One or two of them straight geezers never thieved. Then at the back there was our Sharon. Got to be how they clocked my release, on account of how I never told anyone except Mum. She was all right Sharon, must have reckoned it was cool letting on these.

'Morning Nicky,' they went like school assembly. It had to be they practised it. They were cackling and trying to stop themselves.

'Fuck me,' I turned round and said. 'Fuck me up the railway.'

'Had a good journey?' went Wayne. It had to be something he heard on a video. Journeys round Wayne happened on lifted motors. Got out of Feltham one time lifted the governor's Audi to get home.

'What the fuck this?' I went. 'Orgy crack house or what?'

'Give him the keys Noreen.'

'What?'

Noreen picked up my mitt, put the flat keys in it.

'This is your gaff Nicky,' went Javed.

'What?'

'We all put together Nicky got you a flat,' went Sharon. 'So you never got to come home now and put up with Shithead, and then you can go round Kelly's see the kid when like you want. Anyhow like there it is.'

There was a silence, like only a bit of giggling.

'Fuck,' I went.

They got me a place.

'This some mortgage divvy?' I turned round and said.

'It's straight. Rented. You got a book. A oner a week.'

'Social pay that?'

'We paid four weeks deposit four weeks advance,' went Ricky Hurlock that Noreen's brother passed Maths at school. 'Housing Benefit ought to cough most of that. Take about six months same as usual only the geezer's cool.' Meant they probably sent Ricky and Noreen round negotiating be polite. 'Knows you're on benefit. Housing don't pay enough we make up the difference a while.'

'You geezers put up eight big notes?'

'No problem Nicky we robbed the churches,' went Jimmy Foley. Everyone cackled.

'Jesus.'

They found me a gaff. I never had a gaff in my life. Make a cup of coffee four in the morning you wanted. Lie on the floor eating crisps. Watch *Home and Away*.

I was gobsmacked.

'So there Nicky thassit,' they all went. Then they all pushed the rum round. Then that Noreen went showing me round. Bedroom bathroom sitting room, a recess for cooking. Jesus. Then they all started not knowing what to do next, so they drank their rums and clocked the door.

'Jesus,' I went again.

'Nicky you got to stop saying that like how you know I'm very religious,' went Shelley Rosario. They all cackled on account of how Shelley made her living on the street.

'Geezers,' I went instead.

'All right Nicky,' they cackled again, 'mention it man, see you around.' Then they all finished up and bundled slowly out the door. 'Got to go now Nicky,' went Noreen. Only Sharon was left behind.

I sat down and clocked around the walls. I felt dizzy.

'This your idea Sharon?' I turned round and said.

'Not only me Nicky.'

'Fucking brilliant.'

'I know.'

'Reckoned I was coming out on nothing.'

'Didn't reckon we could let that Nicky after all this time.'

'I owes you Sharon.'

19

'Mention it Nicky. Now how about I show you how everything works eh, cooker and water and that?'

'Fucking all right Sharon. Fucking all right girl.'

So she showed me round, then she went off home, then I made a cup of tea with my kettle they bought me, then I lay down on my bed and got a bit of my sleep.

It was better than being in Wandsworth.

★  ★  ★

Mum was putting the kettle on. She was putting the kettle on when I went away too. Slow cup of tea.

'Ullo Nicky,' she turned round and said.

'All right Mum?'

'Come home for your dinner Nicky?'

'No I got a pattie. You all right Mum?'

'Not bad.'

'He here?'

'Work.'

A result Shithead was at work. Never expected him to take a day off when I came out any road. Mum visited me two weeks before, came through the sentence once a month. Sharon came up and Kelly and the kid and some mates. Then I got one home leave, Sharon and her Kevin babyfather picked me up in his motor. Mum sent the dosh for batteries, a pair of trainers one time. Got to be she nicked it out Shithead's pocket. See her now and you reckon I just popped next door for a bowl of sugar. Or maybe a rock.

'Want a cup Nicky?'

'Don't mind Mum no sugar.'

'No sugar?'

'Cut it out in there. Got to buy it except meals.'

'Waste away no sugar. You stopping Nicky?'

'Got some business get sorted. Report Probation. Sign on. Report up Kelly. See the kid. You heard I got a gaff?'

'Bleeding brilliant Nicky don't ask me how you got mates like that.'

'Find out who your mates are Mum. Some I never smelled since sentence. Some got me this gaff. And that Sharon reckon she got to be a diamond.'

'Leave off,' went Sharon peeling chips.

'Got to be all them drugs I used to give her and the kid.'

Sharon giggled. Mum went shitfaced.

'You keep her out your dirty bleedin' habits she's a clean girl Sharon 'cept she gets up the spout once in a while.'

'Mum! I only got one!'

'Yeah and more luck than judgment you

ask me. You heard who she been seeing lately Nicky?'

'Mum leave off!'

'That Rameez is all.'

'Rameez . . . ' I went. 'Rameez. Jesus Sharon you never spilled that one.'

'You heard about . . . '

'Yeah that George made it his business. Jesus Sharon.'

'Never wanted to spoil your release Nicky.'

So this was what George was leaning on. Reckoned I had to find out soon enough. Reckoned then I had an obligation.

'You friendly that Rameez?'

Sharon gave Mum a quick one, giggled. 'Just like a quick one over the settee now and then eh Nicky,' she went.

Mum spilled some of her tea in the chip pan nearly started a fire.

'Spoils his marriage prospects his accident,' I went. 'First off he maybe only got one eye. Second he mislaid an important finger.'

'Don't be mean,' Sharon giggled.

'Changes a few things though,' I went.

'Like what?'

'Few things that George turned round and said, met me out the station, nothing about a warrant only letting on about Rameez. And a few other bits.'

'You don't get involved now Nicky. Got a

place you want to sleep in it.'

'I aren't getting involved only I better talk up Rameez see what the fuck's going down. Tell you later maybe.'

'Boys' business eh?'

'Something like that. Fuck knows.'

'Search me Nicky, I never knew what this is all over, he never tells me business you know? I only been screwing him is all.'

So then Mum spilled a bit more tea, went 'Shut it that dirty talk you Sharon, can't you kids these days just do it not got to talk about it for Christ's sake?'

So Rameez was putting it up Sharon. No concern of his marriage prospects, we were only kidding up Mum. He'd never get married up Sharon, wrong colour wrong religion, so she was never worrying about his scars. Never helped in general you might say, missing a jam pie and missing a few fingers never did help your marriage prospects in general, only it never concerned Sharon. Mystery to me though what Rameez sussed in Sharon, not even blonde.

More important on my account though was if I owed Rameez due to him screwing my sister. Some point of honour bound to be, far as Rameez clocked it. Fucked if I knew. Complication was if I missed out some point of honour then Rameez gets out of hospital and slices me. Only one way to go you miss out on some point of honour. Sliced.

Best go up Whipps Cross and give some chat round Rameez.

Jesus it was a difficult day. There I was only after some fucking peace and quiet. Now I needed to get up Probation, sign on, round Kelly lived up Aldriche Way now they moved her off the estate. Get up Whipps Cross now in the bargain. Best nick some motor, meant going down Blackhorse Rd tube out the way. First check out no Bill watching, one of their favourites down there. Usually a few Golfs round Blackhorse Rd, and maybe some poxy 205.

'Best get on I got plenty business,' I went.

\*    \*    \*

I left the Golf up the Town Hall car park and reported Probation on my licence no problem. Andy my probation was away probably in the bleeding Channel tunnel as usual so I clocked the duty officer some bird. Chatted a few words with Rosie on reception in the bargain, still there and still turned me down on a few Pernods up some club. Made an appointment for seeing Andy next week.

Walked back up Church Hill to sign on. They made me go up Grosvenor Park Rd. I went up. These days you got paid about a year later after they made you answer fourteen million questions, only the sooner you started the sooner you got the giro. So I booked in on fresh claims and walked back to look up my flat. Just make sure it was still there. Made a cup of tea and used the toilet. Never needed either only it felt good. Washed the cup flushed the toilet, went out again.

Walked back up the Town Hall to pick up the motor then drove up Whipps Cross. They wanted you to stop nicking cars they ought to get a decent bus route up Whipps Cross. Got to go via Southend to get from the Town Hall up the hospital.

Put the Golf in the car park so it got nicked by some other geezer. I used it enough now, and Old Bill watched Whipps Cross car park heavy. Probably be some mate of Rameez's who'd give me a ride back. Otherwise I'd have to hijack some minicab driver, only joking.

I found him guarded, one outside the ward one in front of the bed. Geezer outside asked me who I wanted.

'Rameez,' I went.

'Excuse me sir but I must just give you a quick rub down, you'll understand for security reasons.'

Made me cackle. Last rub down I got was that morning before they let me out, only that time they never went excuse me sir.

I lifted the arms. Then they checked Rameez knew me and wanted me in.

Rameez was in a side ward. His mum was there, making it a bit embarrassing.

'Nicky,' went Rameez.

'All right Rameez? All right Mrs Ahmed?'

'Good afternoon Nicky.' Rameez's dad drove a 97 bus, his mum worked up an Asian lunch club. They were the politest people I ever met. Fuck knows where they got Rameez.

'Well, I must be going,' went Mrs Ahmed. 'Nice to see you looking so well Nicky, I haven't seen you for a long time.' It couldn't be she didn't know where I was, she read the paper like anyone else. 'Rameez, I will be back later on.'

'Thanks Mrs Ahmed,' I went. 'I've been away you see.'

'Yes. Well, I must be going.'

'Thanks Mum,' went Rameez.

She went out.

'Run it by me again Rameez,' I went, 'how the fuck your mum and dad got you? Gooseberry bush job or what? They got nice quiet daughters work hard and sexy in the bargain, then they got a crazy villain like you.'

Rameez cackled. 'Got to have someone bring in the dosh man.'

He looked like shit.

'How do I look Nicky?' he turned round and said.

'Look like shit Rameez sorry geezer only you look like shit.'

'Yeah I know.'

One mince pie was covered up. All round it was blotched, bruised. The other one was wild, scared. One arm was under the sheet. The other one was thin as a poker. He looked like he never ate for two weeks. Tubes came out of the good arm. He looked like shit.

Rameez was one hell of a flash geezer. Used to be.

'You been up our Sharon then?' I went for starters.

He cackled again, a bit gruff. 'We went down the marshes a couple times,' he went.

'Never reckoned she got the hots for you. Still no accounting for taste.' Truth was Rameez scared me shitless even when he was my mate. Would have warned Sharon only I never knew.

'Good of you come and see me Nicky. Got out today eh?'

'You came up on visits Rameez never needed to. Brought me the weed. Took a chance.'

'No problem Nicky. You paid on the nose that bit of work before. You took the agg. And I hope you got a bit put by on that one.'

'Official I'm brassick. Unofficial I got a bit put by. Then they got me a gaff you reckon.'

'I heard.'

'You had a share in that?'

'Little.'

'I owes you.'

'You don't owe me nothing Nicky Burkett. That bit of work you got the sentence was strictly business. Visited you anyone would. Saw your sister ain't got nothing on it. You don't owe me nothing.'

We clocked each other. He was gabbling.

'That bad is it?' I turned round and said.

He just nodded.

Reckoned I had to take a natural to let him get over it. He hid it from his mum, now he was going to blub and sure as hell never wanted me clocking him. Blub out of one eye anyway. I went up the toilet.

I came back and sat there and I turned round and went 'Geezers worse than that business we was in before?'

'Plenty worse Nicky. That time was only drugs. This one's motors.'

'Motors!' I screeched. I never believed it. 'Motors!' I went again till I remembered the

Old Bill, they heard it the same as half the ward except the old deaf ones. Geezers went for his mince pie and half his fingers on account of motors!

'Motors!' I went again more quietly. 'Jesus Rameez they'll be wanting my toes teeth ears never mind them fingers.'

He had to giggle. 'Believe it Nicky,' he went. 'Motors. Only big ones.'

'Got to be fucking flying motors for that.'

'Near as. Fly away out of London right quick.'

'Performance motors? Mercs and BMWs?'

'And Jeeps and Range Rovers and couple Lotus. Roller. Few Porsches.'

'Where you find a Roller up Walthamstow?'

'Up the dog track. Came down Bushey or somewhere, some geezer made a bit on his roofing business. Another Roller up Hoppetts only they reckon that's guarded in a machine gun nest.'

'Give me the story Rameez.'

He stopped a bit. Got a bit of pain here and there only I reckoned I had the answer. I got him a drink. Bit of water, lot of vodka I brought in. Put some weed in his cabinet but put the vodka back in my pocket. Gave him a moment.

'So give me the story Rameez,' I went again.

'Since you went away Nicky. All since you went away. Ringing got very big notes.'

'Export?'

'Ireland, Holland, name it. They get kids nick a Jaguar Sovereign like. Lot of Asian kids fancy the ride. Chances of getting away are about fifty-fifty. They hear the story there's some performance Jag up Hampstead. They get invited to lift it for someone. You clock a lot of Asian kids up Bishop's Avenue though? Not a large bet on getting away. If they do they ride the Jag down the North Circular, up the Lea Valley round some warehouse, then like as not crash it in the warehouse 'cause they can't reach the brake. Hand it over and the kids get a oner, maybe two. Buys a few nights up the Odeon Leicester Square eh Nicky?'

'You done it Rameez?'

'Do me a favour Nicky. I was a broker one or two times. Make the intros you know? Only I'm a geezer due some respect Nicky you reckon that, got a bit too much position for interfering motor vehicles.'

'Sorry Rameez not thinking, mind's elsewhere.'

We sipped his Lucozade with a bit of vodka.

'So them performance motors,' I went, 'they all new or what? I heard they all got

30

alarms and trackers and fuck knows what these days.'

'Alarms you just nuke Nicky,' he went. 'Smash it or fucking take no notice drive off with it. Some of them go off when you turn the key, so you never turn the key. Break the barrel or wire it. Trackers is a problem only most of these motors ain't new so they ain't got one. Or they never buy one, too mean. Even when they got one and even when they catch you it's still only them kids get nicked, never the main man. No problem Nicky.'

'You want a spliff Rameez?' I turned round and said.

'Talking. You my man. Best not let the law see.'

I lit up and opened the window. Smoking wasn't allowed in hospitals I heard.

'So what you got on the rest this business Rameez?' I went. 'You heard DS Grant got it?'

'I heard.'

We cackled.

'Never happen to a better geezer. Only now they offered me Rameez, Old Bill offered me.'

'Offered you what?'

'Offered me a big drink on finding the geezers. And it ain't spelled out only I never be surprised the next contact they just happen to hint I might rub a few out.'

'Rub them out Nicky!'

'Yeah.'

'Jesus Nicky.' He started on giggling again. It seemed like a bit of spliff and this story was the best cure Rameez could get, had him cheered up in no time. 'Pardon me Nicky only how you going to rub someone out?' Giggled again. 'Most you can do cut your sandwich in the morning. We know you finished up on a slaughter only he very near begged you. Old Bill reckon you Jack the Ripper or what? Pardon me Nicky.' Reckoned he might start on the hysterics in a minute. Not very polite really calling me in question. Him an invalid in the bargain.

'Old Bill reckon I got to be a villain anyway got the connections now. They reckon they never find out who plugged a copper only they offer. Maybe offered other geezers dunno.'

Rameez wiped off his tears and I junked the spliff. 'Jesus Nicky,' he went. 'Only I never knew a lot on this just stepped on their toes I reckon. Never knew the whole business. I gained a Jag, new model. Had it hid up waiting my time. They came after it, must have heard I had it away. I went after Mickey Cousins out of north Chingford, big car dealer heard he was around it. Found Mickey by his garage nine at night, only next I knew there was seven of them — none of them him of course, none identified and he was down his club all night. I never knew the muscle, hired help out of Plaistow or somewhere. Me I only got two with me only wanted the motor back. We was in trouble right off. Others scuttled only the help wanted me. They reckoned they were going to give me a lesson on not nicking high performance motors. They were after making a deterrent Nicky, for me or any others. You see the rest.'

'And DS Grant?'

'Fuck knows, I never even clocked him. Tell me it was the same time though. My wager is he started arresting geezers or some such shit, so they sorted him. I was out of it Nicky.'

'And the eye?'

'They reckon they save it Nicky.'

'Yeah? Hey that's fucking great Rameez!'

'They not sure and we maybe not know until a week after they take the bandage off. But they reckon.'

'Fuckin' good news Rameez.'

'Yeah,' he grinned. 'Just hope they don't fuckin' come back is all.'

'You got the law protecting you now.'

He snorted. I snorted.

'And your marriage prospects?' I turned round and went.

He cackled. 'Only a scar Nicky, what's a

33

scar eh? You heard our women back home wear veils? Maybe she never clock the scar till too late eh?'

Seemed not a good chance to me, only best not let him down just a while. We had another little drink then I went off. I was pissed and stoned, Rameez was right out of it. His mum and dad might reckon he made a startling recovery when they turned up an hour later, or they might reckon he was down for a coma.

⋆ ⋆ ⋆

I went up Kelly's so I could clock the kid and maybe get a bit. Couple of times on home leave I got it and then once on special visits when the alarm went. Apart from that I never had it in years. Nearly forgot what it tasted like.

Got a cab over Aldriche Way, where she lived now. Place had about as much soul as a night in Romford.

I went in the wrong building first, deliberate so I could go out again and see who was there. Old habits. There was no-one. I went up the wind tunnels round the buildings, up the stairs and banged on the door.

'All right Nicky?' went Kelly.

'All right Kelly?'

I went in and there was little Danny, not so little now. 'All right Dad?' he went.

'All right Danny?' Then I picked him up hugged him swung him round. He liked that, laughed, shouted, wanted more. So did I. Only I got knackered first.

'You just out today then Nicky?'

'Yeah. You heard they got me a gaff?'

'Yeah Sharon said. Brilliant eh?'

'Fuckin' brilliant . . . '

'Fuckin' brilliant eh?' went Danny.

Chip off the old block my son.

'I wrote you I'd be round tonight,' I went.

'Yeah I got the letter Nicky.'

'So what time does he go to bed then?'

'You only just got here he reckons you'll take him out or something.'

'Oh, right. Where'd you want to go boy? Tell you what, tomorrow I take you down McDonald's eh? Get a milk shake?'

'Fuckin' brilliant Dad,' goes Danny.

'And swimming?'

'Not too bad.'

'Dog track? Bit of clubbing? Only joking. Be here about four then.'

'Say no more Dad you got it.'

Jesus.

So we got a beer and clocked a video and then Danny went off when I said to. Kissed

35

me goodnight. Always did what I said that kid, I always told her she was too soft on him.

'So how you been Nicky?' she went when he got in bed.

'No complaints now Kelly. Be a bit better for a bit of nookie though, touch of the other.'

'Don't know about that Nicky.'

'How'd you mean, wrong time or what? Only I been waiting several years is all.'

'You got it on home leave.'

'Home leave!' I laughed. She had to be winding me up. 'Home leave was years ago eh, now you're having a joke innit?'

'I got a next man Nicky.'

Jesus again.

I sat there and stared.

She stared back. It was for real.

'You mean I been away all them years and you waited and we did it on home leave, only then I come out and you got a next man? Fuckin' roll on Kelly give me a break eh? Get serious woman.'

'I got someone else last week. I reckoned it was best I told you after you got out case you went mental.'

'Jesus Kelly you sent me about four hundred Dear Johns first six months I was in, I never went mental, fuckin' relief you ask me. Then come the time for getting out reckon I could screw you all round Chingford

36

you reckon you found someone else last week.'

'Sorry Nicky. Just the way it happened. Too long to wait I reckon.'

'Fuck me. Danny know?'

'Not yet. Seen him is all.'

'Who is it? Some geezer I know I got to kill him.'

'You just got out for that Nicky. Do yourself a favour don't kill no-one. Barry never done you no harm.'

'Barry? Barry? What kind of a name's Barry?'

'Barrington. Barry for short.'

'Barrington? You serious? He got to be black then?'

'No he's a white geezer Nicky.'

'White geezer name of Barrington? You makin' joke aintcha? He drive a Porsche?'

'Might do. He's a German.'

Jesus.

'This ain't getting no better Kelly,' I turned round and said. 'You fucking a German name of Barrington rides a Porsche. What kind German ponce calls himself Barrington?'

'Well he ain't no dope dealer and he ain't no car thief and he's doing some business course up London on account of the Common Market and he takes me up Charlie Chan's and like buys me presents.'

'Bought you a Porsche?'

'No not yet. Offered to buy me a dog up the stadium though.' She giggled.

'Not the whole fucking stadium?'

'Not this week. Reckon he will though.' Then she started giggling some more then I did too couldn't help it. 'Fucking Barrington,' I went, 'how the fuck you get a kraut name of Barrington Kelly? Not von Barrington I reckon?' Then we both fell about and I went down the road still cackling.

★ ★ ★

I went back up Mum's.

'All right Nicky you're back quick,' she went.

'Quick.'

'You been up Kelly's then?'

'Reckon.'

'Reckon she never gave it you then,' went Sharon giggling, 'you being back that quick and all eh?'

'Now you Sharon none of your filth,' went Mum.

'She got a German geezer,' I turned round and said.

'She got what?'

'She got a German geezer.'

'Jesus. A German geezer. He black an' all?'

'Now Mum,' went Sharon.

'She reckons not. Name of Barrington.'

'Barrington!'

'Barrington!'

'He got to be black.'

'She reckons not. Drives a Porsche.'

'He ain't black then.'

'Jesus.'

'You poor little fucker Nicky . . . '

'Shut that filth Sharon . . . '

'Your Kelly gone and stood you up for a little German fucker name of Barrington drives a Porsche. You ain't got no chance Nicky birds is all the same you ask me. Poke 'em and leave 'em is my advice.'

'What they did to you Sharon I reckon,' went Mum.

'Poke 'em and leave 'em they only want your dosh. Reckon he'll take her flying on his Spitfire?'

'They never had no Spitfires,' went Mum. 'It was our lot got them Spitfires, them Germans got them others.'

'Reckon he takes her round his castle then? Them Germans got a load of lettuce Nicky and what I heard bleedin' great dongers an' all.' Sharon started giggling taking the piss and Mum in the bargain then too. So I had to cackle no choice really. Fucking German up Chingford, lose your bird on a German up

Chingford. Nowhere the foreigners didn't get to these days.

Reckon she'd be back though and panting for it. Soon as he started on telling her his football stories how they kept winning the World Cup, she had to be back. Kelly never could abide football. I never met a German stopped rabbiting about football. Mind you I only ever met them up football matches.

Sharon reckoned she'd take me out so I could buy her a drink out of my discharge.

# 3

Then it all got very busy. All I wanted was a quiet life only it all got very busy.

First I took little Danny out like I promised, show him I was out of the nick and a big man now.

'Hi Dad!' he went when I got in the door, still clocking a video.

'Hi Danny! All right Kelly? Seen any Nazis lately?'

'Germans Nicky.'

'Oh yeah Germans. We off then Danny?'

'Just watch the end of this video Dad.'

'Oh right.' I picked up the box. *Terminator*, that's my boy. We watched the end, then we got his coat on and away down the street.

We got the bus. Not a very big man going on the bus, only that Kelly always reckoned it was immature nicking motors and anyway she never wanted her son in one. And von Barrington never nicked motors. Anyway, yesterday I only lifted one for old times, never stand the excitement these days. Twenty-three years old, slippers and a mug of cocoa.

So we got the bus down the Central. Danny proud as a fart have his dad around.

Me proud as a fart with my son. Fuck 'em, I got my kid.

'Where we going Dad?' he went up the Central.

'McDonald's you want?'

'Oh.'

Quiet a bit while we went on Hoe St. Then he went: 'Dad?'

'What?'

'You care we go up McDonald's?'

'Not if you don't want it son.'

'Oh.'

'Where you want to go?'

'Up the sweet centre Dad.'

'Indian sweet centre?' I stopped ready to go back the other direction.

'Yeah.'

'What you want there get some sweets?'

'Want a moon curry Dad and some of them bargies, all right? Mum says it gets your juices going.'

I nearly walked into the wall outside the Central. Never mind. We went on down past Queen's Rd up near Baker's Arms. Only sweet centre I knew around.

'This suit you son?'

'Wicked Dad.'

'Don't know what they got in here but we find out eh?'

They got plenty of his bargies only not his

moon, but they got a pile of other stuff he scoffed there and then. And in the bargain he ordered a tub of lime pickle. Put it in the middle of the table, kept dipping everything in there. Me it made my eyes water, him he very near drank it. Jesus. I got a six-year-old kid loved his lime pickle. It was evil.

Then we came out so full of grub we were barely walking. Waddled up towards the Central blinking in the sunlight when what did we find but a little problem, just a few feet up the pavement. Mickey Cousins was coming away from Silk's.

★ ★ ★

Now they were both motor traders, Silk's and Mickey Cousins. Only difference was Silk's was legit. Mickey Cousins was about as straight as a helter skelter. But he wore a camel hair coat and he knew a few geezers and he sat in the directors' box up the Orient. Say no more. Then he got a big yard up Chingford and he lived by the forest, and he never bought either of them off his lottery winnings.

I reckoned Mickey Cousins. Normal times he reckoned me like a piece of dirt landed on his collar. Couldn't be there, brush it away.

Me and Danny went to go past.

Mickey stood in our road. Him and his two geezers.

'You Nicky Burkett ain't it?' he went.

Jesus I was tired of this. Geezer blocked you in Wandsworth with no respect it was a battery in a sock in the recess, no messing.

'Fuck off,' I went. 'Just fuck off out my way.'

'Fuck off,' went Danny. 'Just fuck off out his way.'

Strange to tell, Mickey never moved.

'I heard you were keepin' company of police officers,' he goes. 'And you just out of the porridge. Got to be a connection there eh?'

I looked him up. 'You said your piece?' I goes.

'And I'm thinking you ought to be a bit more polite sunshine,' he goes, 'or else my boys here might want to have a few words in your earhole off the street. You got that? You catch my drift? You going to keep out of my flightpath or do you reckon you're the big'un now you did a bit of time? You want your kid here while my boys speak to you or what?'

The geezers stood there looking intelligent.

We had a problem.

Then sudden from behind there came a very nice noise. Very nice noise indeed. 'You got a problem Nicky?' it went. 'Them geezers

44

giving you aggravation? They know they in Walthamstow here?'

It was Javed and Aftab and it was a few of their mates out of Queen's Rd. Mobiles had been very busy two or three minutes. There were Asian kids coming out of all directions, never got a chance to dirty up a camel hair coat before. They stood very close round Mickey and his boys. They were out their league but there were a lot more of them.

Mickey gave me the big stare.

'I'm going home now young man,' he went. 'You'd be best advised to remember what I said is all.' Then he turned round and went.

Danny kept on eating his coconut sweet. 'He fucked off Dad innit?' he went.

★  ★  ★

Next morning I belled George the warrant. Nothing else for it. Got him round his office drinking tea nine in the morning after his rounds. Brought a couple of punters up the cells, had a cup of tea.

'George,' I went.

'Nicky.'

'Something came up George. Need a talking.'

'Go ahead Nicky.'

'I mean like a heavy talking George,

45

meeting. Meet somewhere.'

'Come round here Nicky like most people do, have a chat.'

'Yeah only most geezers ain't just come out of nick not keen on going up the courts again. Bad enough being clocked with a copper, going up court in the bargain got to be brain damage.'

'Leave it out Nicky you're hurting my ears. Just come up and bang on the window, pretend you're a human.'

'Meet you on the North Circular under the Billet six o'clock.'

'Tell you what then Nicky, College Arms six o'clock. You owe me a pint anyway.'

I ignored that. 'Lion and Key up Leyton?'

'You're taking the rise Nicky. If I went up the Lion and Key they'd fumigate. Not the best pub in London to be Old Bill.'

'All right George. College Arms at six. How'll I know it's you?'

'By my face Nicky. If it's someone else's face it ain't me.'

'See you later George.'

★ ★ ★

I went up the Social with my Bl. Yesterday I did the Unemployment. Took about three hours doing what used to take ten minutes,

46

blame the fucking government. Today I took a big newspaper and sat till I saw someone about Income Support and Community Care grant and Crisis Loan and the business. Up the Social these days they very near wanted the truth drug and a DNA test. Still I sat there passed the time, then would you believe it 3.30 they wanted to close up so they gave me a giro. Got to be some kind of miracle. Had a flag I'd have waved it.

Then I went up Wood St to cash it. I bought a can of lager out of Buy Best for passing the time. Had to be getting old, I never bought anything official out of Buy Best in my life. So I got a can of lager and went up the post office. Never even knew why I went up there. Wood St post office you waited so long you were due that pension by the time you got up the counter.

I stood there in the queue thinking about it all, like I'd been doing all day, wondering why the fuck the man was after me. On account of I spoke to the Old Bill? Mickey Cousins got to natter to the Bill himself once in a while, grease a few palms get left alone. Treading on his toes? Maybe so, only I never reckoned where it was I'd been treading on them. No doubt he got an attitude though, no doubt at all.

So I was sipping my lager and giving it

brain. Otherside of the counter I clocked Rafiq, lived near my Mum only he did well. Just before my hair turned white I got served, got my wedge then leaned up the side reading the leaflets till I finished my beer. Never liked supping on the street, no class.

From the leaflets it looked like the post office dealt everything up to a manicure these days. Flog you a stamp and clip your nails.

Then not even an excuse me.

Two geezers walked in. Big thin white geezers reckoned they wanted a few bob and they wanted it over the counter right now. Only they never had their savings books with them. Make it worse they went straight up the head of the queue. Very bad manners only no-one raised an objection. On account of they had shooters.

They both started yelling together. Sounded a bit like Chas & Dave, very noisy.

THIS HERE'S A FUCKING RAID!'

'EVERYONE DOWN! THIS HERE'S A FUCKING RAID!'

'FUCKING DOWN AND SHUT IT YOU FUCKERS! FUCKING DOWN!'

'GET THAT CASH OVER HERE, NOBODY FUCKS UP THEN NOBODY GETS HURT!'

They saw the movie. Same one Danny was watching. They bought the balaclavas. Only then it looked like they bought the shooters out of Toys R Us.

And one of them was pissed.

The fuck were they doing here?

You got used to it when you worked up Wood St post office. Got raided now and then like paying your Council Tax, anyone short of a few readies for their dealer went down and raided the post office. Only these geezers were never serious. Two of them for a start was never enough. One of them rat-arsed. Both of them on the video and pushed up their balaclavas due to the heat. Were they independent or some big man's toy soldiers? Someone's geezers they were going to be very unpopular when they got back to the office.

It was getting very noisy in there got to admit. There were women screaming and the two geezers shouting and waving their things. Only the staff were cool, a bit bored. I still stood over the corner clocking the leaflets wishing I was down the boozer.

'YOU GIVE OVER THAT FUCKING CASH! DON'T YOU GO NEAR THAT ALARM YOU FUCKER!'

I never recognised them, not Walthamstow or Leyton far as I knew. Nor south London, you only came out of Peckham this far when you were pros and these were never pros. Out of Stratford maybe. Bad manners though coming up our manor taking our dosh.

Then Rafiq pulled me standing in the corner minding my business.

'Nicky,' he went quiet, 'you see them shooters?'

'What you say Rafiq?'

'You think them shooters are for real or is it you think that geezer nearest you is holding a water pistol?'

I clocked it. It was a water pistol.

'He got a water pistol,' I went. 'Might shoot that water out hard Rafiq but still only a water pistol.'

There was still shouting and yelling going on down the far end and now they were getting out the cash. Rafiq had to speak up.

'Nicky,' he went loud, 'you see my mum over there getting into trouble just like always?'

Then I recognised her. Little old Asian woman shaking her finger at the rat-arsed one, probably giving him a piece of her mind, not very wise. 'There is no need to speak like that,' I heard her turn round and say.

'FUCKING FUCK OFF!' he went shoving her on one side.

Always was the same Rafiq's mum, always getting in there never taking time out. Years ago accused my mum nicking her four pints semi-skimmed milk off her doorstep. Fucking ridiculous we never used semi-skimmed. Anyway turned out it was Wayne Sapsford's little brother Clark, drank four pints the way to school. So first off my mum and Rafiq's mum had a scrap outside Walthamstow nick when she made the allegations, then they went off bingo together when the pigs gave them the news on the big villain.

'Nicky,' went Rafiq. Then he passed me a baseball bat across the counter. 'Nicky, you just like to slap that bastard please while he isn't looking? Do it myself you understand but you can see I can't get over the counter.'

'Who me?'

'Yes you just like to bop him please? Not on the head you might kill him. Just tap him in the belly or somewhere, stop him bothering my mum.'

'You sure you can't get over that counter?'

'Sure sure. Anyway it against regulations.'

I picked up the baseball bat. Rat-arse was only a couple of paces off, and still shouting like four geezers while they bagged up the paper. I stepped up to him. Shit. Got nothing against the feller, trying to do a bit of work, only if Rafiq's mum got hurt and I stood by I was going to get murders off my mum.

I had the butt in my mitt and the end in my palm. Very very sudden I shoved the big end hard and deep in the geezer's belly. He went down with a whoosh.

Then I gave the bat back Rafiq right quick. It went a lot quieter too without him yelling and screaming. The other geezer turned round and all he knew was his mate was out gasping on the floor, sudden attack of stomach cramp maybe from all that shouting.

'The fuck happened?' he yelled.

'The fuck the matter with you Gal? The fuck going on?'

Gal rolled about whooshing. Never turned round and said a lot.

Then his mate knew the Bill got to be on their way soon, what with the delay and someone bound to have pressed the alarm. He got very unfriendly about that and very sudden there was a crack and a whizz and the plaster went tumbling. Jesus Christ. Maybe Gal had a water pistol only his mate never.

'Rafiq?' I went. 'You see what I see Rafiq?'

'Very sorry Nicky, very very sorry. Truly I never thought either of them had a gun. You could have got killed man taking action like that.'

Jesus.

Then thank fuck the geezer fucked off leaving Gal and the money behind, and just after that the Old Bill turned out.

I found George snout deep in some pint of black stuff I never even smelled before.

'The fuck's that George?' I went.

'Brown ale Nicky. Put hairs on your goolies lad.'

'Fuckin' roll on George I ain't sure it's safe drinking next to that. You sure it ain't radioactive?'

'Better than farting out all that fizzy muck you drink. Spose you want a pint of lager?'

'Pint of Pernod please George.'

'Pint of lager!' he goes.

'Cheers.'

We sipped them back. Least he sipped. I never wasted time while I got a freeman's off the Bill.

'How's the missis George?' I went polite like.

'Mustn't grumble.'

'How's them old fines coming in then eh?'

'Fair to middling.'

'How's Securicor getting on up the court I heard they took half your job over innit?'

'Fucking government want stringing up.'

We sipped and that a bit more.

'Now Nicky this is where I fade out of the picture,' he goes.

'Eh? That stuff radioactive for sure? You

about to dissolve?'

'I'm just here doing the introductions like Nicky, being the messenger, then I don't want no more part of it. My colleagues they just asked me to assist because I knew you and, like, because you've been known to speak to me civil once in a while.'

'Bleedin' have to change that then. Get me a bad rep.'

'So there's someone coming here in a few minutes who'll explain what this co-operation is all about.'

'Co-operation? What co-operation George? I never said nothing about no co-operation.'

'You're here ain't you?'

'Just a talking George just a talking.'

'And I heard you've been round the hospital visited Rameez . . .'

'So?'

'And you found out he's been seeing your sister no doubt . . .'

'So?'

'So you reckon you've got to look after your Sharon's boyfriend, see him right.'

'Just you run your mouth, George mate, just you run your mouth, see me get lit up I don't reckon. Rameez, yeah I went to clock him, pay my respects, never meant I oil his wheels for him. Fucker got carved up, never meant I'm responsible for him.'

54

'So I think I'll leave you now Nicky because I do believe I can see my man approaching. Nicky, this is DS TT Holdsworth, Chingford CID. TT, this is Nicky Burkett.'

Distance of over 150 miles I might not tag him CID. Only other option was gangster. Thick neck shiny trousers leather jacket short hair rough shave and little piggy eyes. CID say no more.

'So you're Nicky Burkett?' he went.

A blonde bit across the bar was giving me the eye I reckoned.

'I'm Martin Holdsworth. They call me TT.'

She got two fine tits, better than anything he got to look at.

'They call me that because I go scrambling. Taking the piss like.'

I swore she rolled her tongue round her lips at me.

'That lager you've got there?'

I tipped it up.

'Pint of lager!' he goes waddling up the bar, everyone in the shop marks him CID. Then all of a sudden she sticks one finger up at me.

'You may have heard I got some business for you if you're interested,' he goes settling down with the drinks again.

What she do that for? This some new thing started while I was away? Meant she got the hots for me couldn't wait to take her knickers down?

'Come over in the corner here Nicky so we can have a quiet word.' Jesus, a quiet word with the filth. My rep was in injury time here.

We settled down all over again. Then I realised the bastard moved me out of her line of vision. 'Let's start at the beginning, shall we?' he went all smarmy, like they do in interview after they beat you brainless in the van. Interview went on record.

'Let's start at the beginning. You might be able to help us, we might be able to help you. I know that discharge grant don't buy many spliffs, eh?' Mr Matey, speak the language.

'You heard about DS Grant of course Nicky?'

'Funny no-one ever got a first name for DS Grant,' I goes. 'Except fucking of course.'

'Don't suppose you ordered any flowers.'

I started on the new lager.

'Well, DS Grant got killed like you know, and feelings get running very high indeed when a copper gets murdered. Some of the lads, not only are they very keen on getting this sorted, they also reckon they might put their hands in their pockets for it.

'Shortage of information so far Nicky, severe shortage of information. So much is obvious to anyone who wants to see, but we ain't got the next connection yet. Bound to come of course, bound to come, only this might be where you come in you understand.'

'I come in? Where the fuck I come in to this?'

'Well, like I said Nicky we know you might be a bit short of the old cash here, and we reckon your ear's got to be close to the ground, bound to hear the whispers.'

'Oh yeah? And if I don't want to hear no fuckin' whispers, only want a bleedin' quiet life for fuck's sake?'

'And of course you know your mate Rameez was involved, in fact DS Grant probably saved him from something very nasty indeed, you heard that?'

'Leaving aside Rameez ain't my mate,' I went, 'like where's he fit in your frame then?'

'Like I said, it was DS Grant stopped Rameez getting terminated, very likely. They were treading on the same toes Nicky, creeping on the same carpet. Rameez went to put his views to some big people, then he found they were a bit too big for him. DS Grant was probably watching the same people, we don't know, then he stepped in and played the hero to save Rameez getting both his eyes put out. But he got plugged.'

'Goodbye DS Grant.'

'The picture. They just wanted to warn

Rameez, warned him a bit heavy. DS Grant was too dangerous to leave, that's how we see it.'

'So go ask Rameez your questions copper. Why you asking me?'

'Rameez? Make me laugh. He might talk to God maybe although only if he got a good offer. Anyway, even if he did he wouldn't be any use to us. Bleeding unconscious wasn't he, little Asian fucker.'

Nice to be taken into the police confidence. Nice to be trusted. Nice to know it was all sweetness before they decided on how they were going to shaft you.

'So we got together, me and the lads, private arrangement, and we thought we might put a drink up for any big news that came our way Nicky. Big big news you understand.'

'How much?'

'Well . . . maybe 2K we were thinking.'

'2K! Fucking Ada, you expect some geezer to get plugged for 2K! You're havin' a laugh aintcha' you're making joke here.'

'We reckon your ear's got to be close to the ground Nicky like I said, and we reckon you might pass me some information once in a while if you hear anything.'

'Oh yeah? And why me so especially? Nothing to do with me just getting out after a

58

manslaughter eh? Nothing like you reckoned I might get off on topping geezers? You tell that George Marshall you found two big ones so I could waste someone? Not very fucking likely I reckon.'

'Good God mate we don't want anything like that,' he went, all of a sudden reckoned I had a tape somewhere. 'Like I said, all we were wanting was some important information which might lead us to the arrest of one or more suspects for this vicious murder of an officer of the law.' Came out of the manual, that bit.

I sat there and clocked my lager. There I was, did my time, came out on jam roll, got a nice new gaff courtesy of my mates, got the chop off that Kelly no bad deal, noshed a smart curry or two and looking about for a new bit of stuff. Got a few bob put away. All hunky-dory in a T-shirt. Then along comes fucking DSTT Holdsworth and his motor-bike reckons I ought to start asking questions off geezers that poke your porkies out or when you get awkward plug you for a terminal. In the bargain he puts out the feelers for whether I like killing a few. For two fucking big ones.

'You got to be a penny short,' I went. 'Know the big dosh ain't about no more off the Regionals, only me get shafted for two big ones? Leaving aside I want a quiet life, you got to be mental.'

'We could get you half of that just for a finger on someone. Then again we can always give you the protection you know, a change of ID and a flat up Willesden somewhere.'

'I don't want no change of ID you great pillock, no problem being Nicky Burkett this far. And least of all I don't want no fuckin' flat up somewhere other side of Australia, Jesus. And you reckoned I was a grass now for you and your mates putting up a big drink?'

'That and your mate Rameez getting gouged.'

'Jesus copper he ain't my mate can't you credit that?'

'Very friendly with your sister so I heard.'

'So he's very friendly with my sister. Very friendly with my mum and my grannie and the fuckin' lollipop lady for all I care. You got that?'

'All right Nicky no problem. Just let me give you my card though in case you have a change of mind or in case you might hear anything you think you might like to pass on any time.'

'Card? I'm paying my taxes for cards you bastard, how long is it the fuckin' CID got calling cards?' I was shocked.

'Pay for it myself Nicky. Professional

attitudes pay dividends I find. Let me give you my card.'

'Jesus. Another pint of lager be more use. Goes on expenses no doubt on that eh.'

He got another pint of lager. Then he pissed off. The card went *DS TT Holdsworth, CID Chingford, tel 0181 529 8666.* Then there was his mobile and his home number, only he cut both them off before it came my way. Along with the bit down the bottom. *Always at your service.*

Particularly you wanted a good kicking up the cells any time.

I turned round and searched for the blonde bit. Only she was gone. Sat and wondered why she gave me the finger. Ah, fuck it.

# 4

I belled Jimmy Foley to take me up
Wandsworth to see Slip. Last part of my
sentence Slip was my cellmate.

Slip never liked prison. He never liked the
sentence he never liked Wandsworth he never
liked the screws and most of all he never liked
the food. About five hundred other things he
never rated high on the clapometer either
only they were the starters. Three days after
he arrived he still never ate never spoke never
shit. Then when he started speaking he
carried on like I was never as popular as
Malcolm X either. Far as he was concerned,
prison was a big interruption in his plans and
it never compared with drinking rum and
coke with some totty on some beach in
Jamaica. So he got an attitude.

Then when he started yacking, total change
of plan and he reckoned I was part of his
future. Reckoned I could make up for his
temporary hitch doing two years for importation. All I wanted was to direct his operations
for him while he was away, sit on some
computer set up his cargo flow from Brixton
to Burundi.

Me I played it cool, let him run on.

Jimmy Foley got two advantages for taking me over to Wandsworth. First he could lift a motor for getting there with. Straight out of nick I never wanted a recall for TDA so I was catching buses, only you never could catch buses to Wandsworth, still be standing there. Jimmy nick a motor and we get stopped I could plead not guilty to Allowing To Be Carried, turn round and say I reckoned it was legit, be fighting the case two years.

Second advantage with Jimmy was he got last in the queue when they gave out the Einsteins. Preferred doing every tiling you told him instead of starting on that thinking, hurt his ears. Once he got the serious hump after he got shot on my account, still he mellowed out after and got sweet again. So I belled him to take me up Wandsworth.

I took my Visiting Order felt a bit strange. They let you in then they let you out again, not what I was used to. This time not travelling in a sweatbox either.

Screws all clocked me straight off.

'Fuck me if it ain't Burkett 359,' went shithead on the metal detector at the gate.

'Mr Burkett to you Sunshine,' I went. 'And I ain't bringing in no drugs so none of them body searches give you a feel up.'

'Don't do body searches at this nick on

visitors unless they give grounds for suspicion. Only you've never come on visits from the outside so you wouldn't know about that.'

'Just let me the fuck in.'

We went through the doings, emptied pockets and took our coats off then put them all in the machine. Never showed up any Armalites even Semtex. Waited in batches of ten, got a quick rubdown and that was security. We got out of the gatehouse across the yard and in the main building.

Walked up the screws' table in visits. 'Fuck me if it ain't Burkett 359,' went the screw on the table.

'Fuck me if it ain't officer Ballocks,' I went. Mr Baldock known as Ballocks. Not such a bad geezer matter of fact, smuggled snout in for a bit of wedge since they cut down on overtime.

They gave us a table number and we waited half the afternoon then Slip came out from the back.

'My man!' he goes.

'My man!' I goes.

'My man!' he goes.

Go on for ever like this. 'This here's Jimmy,' I turned round and said, 'name you put on the VO. Nicked an Astra bring us up here.'

'Yo Jimmy.'

'Geezer.'

'What you want off the canteen Slip?'

'Four Twix two apples three crisps four biscuits one Mars three teas two coffees.'

'You sure you can't gob more than that?'

'Do for a start, only get forty minutes some times you know.'

We settled down sent Jimmy off for the grub. 'And watch them WVS Jimmy,' I goes. 'Scam you off the top soon as look at you thieving cows.' Always could wind Jimmy up.

'You all right Slip?' I went. Looked no fatter, trying to see he could get through the sentence without eating prison food.

'Cool cool. Been allocated Highpoint few weeks.'

'Shithole Highpoint you want Downview or The Mount Slip. Highpoint's a shithole. They got cooking The Mount, you do your rice and peas.'

'Tell me that Lester Piggott went Highpoint got to be good enough man.'

'Yeah and got out on Sunday, only geezer ever got out of nick on Sunday. And you got a stable twenty miles down the road Highpoint's handy, only you ain't then it ain't. You ain't got no stable round Newmarket you keeping quiet about Slip I don't suppose?'

'True words brother. Still I going there now.'

'Get on D wing you can. Nice little open unit. Talk about closing it only I heard it still there. Nip out fish and chips Saturday nights and down the boozer.'

'Hear Nicky, they reckon Spring Hill Saturday nights on the gangster wing they get Chinese delivered know what I mean?'

We ran on about nicks we knew. Usual stuff. Jimmy came across with the grub off the WVS.

Sure enough I marked their cards. 'Thieving bleedin' tarts,' he went. 'Fuckin' old bats chipped me 2p on the coffee then tried rumping me on the change fuckin' cows.' Jimmy got to be the only geezer you could rattle his cage on the WVS, never failed.

Slip fed up on the goodies. 'So when we do the business?' he went in swallows.

'Best now. End of visits they expect it.'

'How we do it?'

'Well normal you get a bird in Slip, give her a tongue job. I prefer I don't kiss you Slip, could start a riot.'

'Fuck me man don't need it that bad.'

'Mars Bar.'

I unwrapped the Mars, took a chew and passed the stuff out of behind my teeth. Cannabis resin I heard it was illegal. Glad to get rid of that silver foil in the bargain. Took it out with the Mars, wrapped them together left it on the table. Slip took a note out of under his watchband. Passed it across nice and easy. Was a fifty. 'Now you keep that right safe in my savings Nicky eh?' he went.

'Jesus Slip how'd you get a half in here?'

'Was hard man. Did the deals in small then some dude back from open he had a fifty. Changed me up.'

Few minutes later he took the Mars and passed the block behind his teeth. Not a lot only enough to keep a few geezers happy a few days.

'Cool Nicky my partner.'

'Decent gear.'

'Only now why you ain't brought me no nice cool chick up partner? Some nice shiny blonde white chick? Maybe you ain't got no sister no more? No cousins? Me and you's partners innit?'

'Brought you Jimmy instead.' I cackled.

'Huh.' He turned up Jimmy. 'Hold nothing on you man only you ain't no shiny white blonde bird know what I mean?'

'Me I ain't no bird correct,' went Jimmy. 'Only I heard you got women screws in here now don't need no more woman.'

Women screws. I reckoned one moment maybe Slip was having a seizure.

Then he cried out.

'Woman!' he went. 'I want she!' Then he started on the Twix. 'You tell me you got a sister Nicky?'

'Come here do business Slip you reckon,' I turned round and said. 'Birds ain't good for business you have to know.'

'Fuckin' too right I suppose man.' He thought on it. 'Fuckin' too right man. Business we get to business. You got my Jamaica all figured yet my friend?'

'Jamaica? Reckoned we were going up Senegal on your count.'

'*You* were going up Senegal Nicky. *You* were going up there on account of you speaks the French and I is otherwise engaged.'

'So what happened?' I was confused. Nothing new though only I was confused. Last few weeks of sentence all he did that Slip was bend my lughole how we were sitting on a load of lettuce exporting computers up his ancestors round Senegal. Buy one here one and a half, sell it round Africa four to five. No problem john. Only connection Jamaica was he got lifted on a Jamaica export licence bringing in the weed in boxes of coconuts.

'So what happened?' I went. 'Been out five minutes and you got a whole new plan here Slip.'

'Ah yes,' he went. 'Ah yes Nicky man I

believe I may have omitted to mention my change of plan.'

'I believe you fuckin' may.'

'Ah yes. You see it may be necessary to make interim plans. Eventual the great scheme is still for the making of a business round Senegal you dig. Only first we build the foundation. I been thinking.'

'Do too much of that thinking,' went Jimmy.

'I been thinking. We need to build up the business, lay the foundations, make the contacts, establish our business plan and *modus operandi.*'

'The fuck's one of them?'

'I been reading up. The book tells you got to have a business plan and *modus operandi*, so them is exactly what we goin' to get you understand.'

'Slip you the mastermind here.'

'My grancestors still waiting in Senegal you dig, only maybe we got to lay the groundwork here.'

'That the same as that other thing?'

'So I got interim plans, get you in the way of being a capitalist bastard established before we make it round Africa. You cool?'

'Cool yeah.'

'So these interim plans they about Jamaica. You get a Jamaica import/export licence and I get you established a merchant before I get out this place.'

I choked on my biscuit.

'Scuse me Slip,' I went. 'Scuse me for mentioning it and spoil this little party, only you forgot you got a Jamaica export licence and what you finished up in here remember? You brought in them little coconuts filled with the weed and the man lifted you at lunchtime, oh pardon me while I have my sandwich first then I reckon you have a import problem. No?'

'Nicky,' he went weary, 'I do believe you made your point maybe two million times or maybe three million when we was in a cell together. Now I don' want to listen up your point further. You have you desire to learn from the past. Point is different. You is legit. You become trader imports exports. Only way we know doing this is Jamaica on account of I know the markets for trade. I is sleeping partner. And thinking partner. Then when I is released I joins you seeing as how them shortsighted bastards no more allow me my own licence. We now is already a trader import export so we finds the market on Senegal simple eh?'

Me it was depressing.

'So how I go about doing all this? I ain't no brains Slip. And Jimmy here he ain't top of the class neither, fact he ain't in the class even.'

'Even,' went Jimmy.

'Me I does the thinking,' went Slip. 'You does three things.' He went dramatic, leaving pause for effect.

'Get pissed? Put it up some tart? Buy a BMW?'

'First you find out becoming a merchant. I give you the address of the British Overseas Trade Board. Second you goes out to Jamaica. I shows you where it is on the map. Third you find out about exporting and importing, check out the market see they want the product man.'

'What product that?'

'Two products brother. Product out of Jamaica you bring coffee . . . '

Then it hit me.

'Eh? Eh?' I goes.

'Eh? Eh?' goes Jimmy.

'I goes to Jamaica?' I goes.

'You goes plenty soon,' he goes. 'Product don't come on its own you got to fetch it.'

'Jesus.'

'Jesus,' goes Jimmy. 'And Mary.'

'And this product what I take out to Jamaica what them Jamaica geezers can't keep their mitts off?'

'No problem.'

'No problem. No fuckin' problem you sat in here Slip. What I take across then?'

'Deckchairs Nicky. They ain't got no deckchairs in Jamaica.'

Jesus Christ Almighty.

★ ★ ★

We went back up the Astra. Some fucker smashed in the quarterlite and had the stereo away. Trouble with Astras everyone wanted bits. Meant we never had any music going home.

'Poxy fuckin' tealeafing bastards,' went Jimmy, 'you can't put nothing down. Lift another one out of Halford's?'

'No matter we be dumping it anyway.'

'True.'

We went off up Trinity Rd round Clapham Common way.

'So this Slip,' went Jimmy, 'he got all his buttons done up? His eggs got scrambled early on or what?'

I cackled. 'Got to be my mate Jimmy,' I went. 'He my mate.'

'Yeah only I your mate too Nicky only I never reckoned you got to go up Jamaica or that place in Africa. Jamaica long way off Nicky you hear. Fuckin' gangsters Jamaica.'

'So what you reckon the plan?'

'Plan?'

'What you reckon the plan?'

'Plan?'

Jesus.

'What you reckon retailing deckchairs round Jamaica?'

'Fuck me Nicky what you reckon I reckon? You start retailing them deckchairs round Jamaica them gangsters gonna get your little short and curlies and mash them right up man.'

'Sherry McAllister's mum,' I went. 'She Jamaican.'

'Maybe.'

'Paulette James's mum and dad they Jamaican.'

'Maybe.'

'You reckon they gangsters?'

'Yeah.'

We cackled both. 'Fuck off Jimmy,' I turned round and said. 'And anyway you reckon them gangsters got a closed deal on that deckchair market Jimmy? Do me a favour it ain't got a lot of hard cash know what I mean?'

We went over Tower Bridge at sixty, sudden clearing.

'Can't all be gangsters round Jamaica. So give me the knockings. You reckon it a bum deal selling deckchairs round Jamaica or you reckon it a slice?'

He hawked up.

'So why you say the gangsters want to mash us up?'

He gave it thought. Hear him ticking. Then he gave it more thought.

Then he went 'All right Nicky so you were always smart did all that French at school. So I don't know why they mash you up. Maybe they just mash you up 'cause they get vex man, I heard them Jamaican gangsters get very vex. Don't like the way you sip your rum punch, mash you up good style so I heard. That how you heard it Nicky too or you heard them's all pussycats these days them Yardies?'

'And you reckon they're into that coffee in the bargain?'

'Maybe they don't like the way you sip that coffee either Nicky, gun you down, fucked if I know.'

'No that coffee export Jimmy, what you say about that?'

'Fuck knows Nicky it confused me. Reckon I'd try Iceland, I never heard tell of gangsters up there. Take them deckchairs up Iceland.'

'Jimmy you want to go up Jamaica with me?'

'Nicky you got to be crazy. Two white boys? Dealing goods in Jamaica? Now I know why my mum always warned me off you, you just totally out of it man, lost the plot goodstyle.'

'So why you reckon my mum warned me off you too Jimmy? Six years old reckoned you were a villain?'

'They were both right then eh?' We cackled again, overtook on the inside down Mile End Rd and shot a grannie light.

'You reckon they could use them deck-chairs Jimmy?'

'They got loungers Nicky. You heard the man say they got loungers. Never be seen dead in a deckchair when they all got loungers.'

'Loungers them big long things?'

'Yeah they got them up Canvey Island, fold out about thirty-eight bits. Birds lounge on them, why they're called loungers. Jesus Nicky you got to know them things, you never come across them when you were out speaking Froggie?'

'Never give it much thought Jimmy tell you the truth. Never clocked any round Calais, neither deckchairs nor loungers. Never went down no beach though, could be why.'

'They still make them deckchairs Nicky? My grannie got one in her garden about a hundred years old. They still make them you reckon?'

'Fuck knows Jimmy. Got to find out I

suppose. And a few more bits besides.'

'Few more bits. You got to be mental Nicky, you lost it when you were in there man. Never even think about it.'

We took the A102 at ninety. Soon be home dump the motor.

★ ★ ★

There was a knocking on the door downstairs.

Took no notice me. Clocking the TV on the settee, could be the licence people.

It went on. Then there were stones on the window. Someone wanted me and reckoned I was there.

I leaned out the window. 'You brought the Chinese?' I went, case it was the law.

'It's me Nicky,' went the voice.

Jesus it was Noreen Hurlock and I was locking her out. Only the most welcome piece in town and got a job in the bargain and I was locking her in the cold.

I was down there opening the door.

'You come by me visiting Noreen?' I went. 'Passion got the better of you then eh?'

'Thought I'd come and see you were all right,' she went.

I reckoned I might faint. Noreen Hurlock wanted to see I was all right.

'You want tea or coffee or tequila or a bit of a bundle on the settee?' I went. I was nervous, grant it.

'Give over Nicky you never change do you?'

'So which you want first?'

'Tea please Nicky and a bit of tequila.'

'No coffee no bundle?'

'They're supposed to come after dinner Nicky, you haven't offered me dinner yet.'

'I got toast.'

'So I brought a curry with me in case you fancied any.'

'You never!'

'I did too.'

'How'd you know I was in?'

'I didn't.'

'Well knock me over. Hang on I got two forks somewhere Noreen and a plate. You bring another plate?'

'No afraid not.'

'Hold it here's a bowl.'

So we took it out the bag she brought it in and we dished up. Then we gobbed it. We drank half a bottle tequila and lime and clocked the TV. It was like being married. Except it was quiet.

'Now I make the coffee,' I went when the movie finished. 'Then we have a little rub-up?' Tell the truth I was shaking so bad a cocktail was easier than a coffee.

'You're such a romantic aren't you Nicky? I've got to be at work in the morning.'

'I could make it quick.'

'You won't be making it anyhow tonight Nicky.'

'Oh.' Then I went 'You heard that Kelly gave me the shove Noreen?'

'Yes I heard,' she went.

We clocked a bit more TV and sipped that tequila. Parked on the settee so we were near as touching.

'Mind you,' she went, 'in certain circumstances.'

'Eh?'

'I might . . . consider . . . '

'Circumstances what circumstances? Jesus Noreen what circumstances? What you consider?'

'You got to do one or two things . . . '

'What?'

'Few conditions . . . '

'Jesus Noreen spill it woman, you consider a bunk-up in conditions? Nick you a yacht? Take you up the dogs? Anything for you Noreen you know that.'

'Not so much a bunk-up Nicky or a rub-up, more a lovemaking. A long slow lingering lovemaking.'

This was ready for nightmare material.

'Christ Noreen, bunk-up, lovemaking anything you bleedin' fancy. Only what
conditions? Never on Saturdays? Standing
on my bonce? You name it Noreen.'

'No nothing like that.'

We waited. Maybe I had a heart attack.

'You know you always made you fancied
me Nicky?'

'Just a touch Noreen just a tiny touch on
account of you're the most beautiful bit of
. . . you got such a sweet personality eh?'

'But there were always a few things you
needed to sort out in your life Nicky you
know before a girl like me might want to be
seen with you, you think of that?'

'Eh?'

'So there might be these few conditions for
you to consider Nicky to see if you thought it
was worth it you know?'

We were here about half an hour ago.

'Just three conditions for now.'

I took a gulp of tequila reckoned it might
help.

'One. You give up crime.'

Jesus.

'Two. You take an Aids test.'

Christ.

'Three. Afterwards you wait two months to
be all clear.'

And the Holy Ghost.

'Noreen . . . ' I went.

'How does that sound to you Nicky?'

'Be drawing my pension Noreen . . . '

'I ain't joking Nicky. Wouldn't be round here unless I meant it you know.'

'Know that Noreen.'

'You want I give you a little kiss Nicky before I go, get us both going a bit see what it might be like?'

'Yeah.' I was speechless shitless. 'Yeah.'

So she gave me a little kiss. Only she started it unusual round my belly, pulled up the T-shirt and sucked on the belly button. Made me go 'ah!' very sudden. Then she moved up pressing up against me so I felt every inch her tits on me then her belly on where she just kissed me and then she put her leg up beside me on the settee. Then she licked her little tongue round my neck and up by my lughole then she bit me on the hooter believe it! 'Ah!' I went again. Then she went licking all round outside my mouth. Gasping by now I was gasping.

Then she got up and gave a little wave and she was gone.

And I was gasping.

*HAVE A GO HERO BEATS OFF ARMED THUGS IN WOOD ST POST OFFICE SIEGE!*

*Walthamstow Guardian* trussed me up proud, like a turkey anyone felt a grievance.

'*Nicky Burkett, 23, was released from prison only last week. Living proof that rehabilitation does happen, Nicky was visiting Wood St post office to buy a second class stamp*' — told them that, better than drink a can of lager — '*when the post office was held up by masked and dangerous armed robbers. Single-handed, unarmed Nicky disarmed one of the robbers through sheer force of personality*' — I never wanted Rafiq fingered on the baseball number — '*and left him ready and willing to give himself up to the law. The other thug made good his escape shortly before the police arrived, but it is hoped that he will be apprehended swiftly.*

'*Modest Nicky said afterwards 'It was nothing special. The boys were trying to do a little bit of work, and got unlucky. Happen to anyone.'*'

★   ★   ★

Mobile got hectic. It rang seven in the morning.

'Is that Nicky Burkett?' it went.

'Jesus.'

'Is that Nicky Burkett?'

'What time you got?'

81

'Seven o'clock. You're Nicky Burkett aren't you?'

'Who wants to know?'

'This is Marie Lewis from the *Sun*.'

'Rising Sun?'

'The *Sun*. Newspaper.'

'Eh?'

'This is the *Sun* Nicky, we want to ask you about the post office siege, maybe we'll do a feature on you and buy your story.'

'The *Sun*?'

'Yes Nicky.'

'You can fuck off then.'

'What? We can pay . . . '

'*Sun's* a fuckin' racist comic.' Knew what the black cons all reckoned to the *Sun*. 'So you can fuck off.'

'But Nicky, er, I heard you were white, isn't that right?'

I switched off.

Few minutes later it went again. 'Mr Burkett, this is Helen Robinson from the *Independent*.'

'No it ain't it's the fuckin' *Sun*. You can fuck right off.' Switched off again and went unobtainable.

★ ★ ★

Then I got up and made the tea. Only good part getting woken up by some fucker off the

*Sun*, it gave me more time enjoying my gaff. Still half awake I made a pot, staggered round, sipped it, sat down on the chair and clocked the world out the window.

Didn't look very friendly, the world.

All I reckoned I wanted was a bit of blue sky and a cup of tea and not being banged up. Now I got all three of them only it never looked very friendly out there. Sitting over the road and up the street was Old Bill, unmarked.

Sitting there in a personal Audi, not even an Old Bill unmarked motor. Seven in the morning, two of them in uniform reckoned they were invisible.

One of them got a big man's uniform on. Not your regular flatfoot. Type they brought out for meeting the queen. Chief Superintendent.

He never lived on our street. Not a superintendent street. So what was his game?

He was observing. Observing my gaff. Only why the fuck would a superintendent want to be doing that?

They sat there a while then the motor moved off and I finished my tea.

# 5

Just coming out for a bit of breakfast on Hoe St I ran in Dean Longmore. Got a new jacket on.

'Yo Dean,' I goes.

'Yo Nicky you lookin' sharp man.'

His jacket got a red stripe down each side.

'You been paintin' Dean?' I goes.

'Eh?'

'Only wondered you painted that stripe on. You in the dosh?'

'Packin' it Nicky. Packin' it. I gone legit.'

'Yeah.'

'Straight up I gone legit.'

Dean Longmore gone legit. Dean Longmore who got born on a visit to his dad in the Ville.

'Dean,' I went, 'shut the fuck up will you and tell me where you lifted that vest.'

'Nicky I gone legit. I got an income and that.'

'And income tax you got? You paying income tax on that income?'

'Don't get fuckin' silly Nicky. Only I earning legit. Motors legit.'

'You winding me up. How in fuck would

you be earning legit?'

'Lassoing. And fetching.'

Fucking smartarse. Go away for a couple years and they all talk a different language.

'You a cowboy?' I went.

'You want a lager?'

'Fuckin' nine in the morning Dean do me a favour. Get a coffee.'

We went in the breakfast.

'That lassoing can't beat it,' he went.

I gave him the look.

'You reckon them old motors get abandoned, Fiats and Datsuns and Carltons?' he went.

'Reckon.'

'And you reckon the Council shoves a sticker on tows them off a week later?'

'Reckon.'

'So before they tows them away you tows them away. Wreck them up some yard for a quarter they give you. These days some of them yards want the logbook only there's always others. Wreck them, they give you some bits make two profits. Easy peasy.'

'Easy peasy.'

'Or even you don't wait on a sticker. You look round some heap, clock there's dirt under, ease it away.'

'And some geezer only likes taking his motor out Sundays in August?'

'Report it nicked get the insurance.'

I drank the coffee.

'Dean,' I goes, 'you ain't never got that jacket out of wrecks.'

'Only then there's the fetching.'

'Fetching.'

'You reckon out of Spain.'

'Spain. I been away Dean you reckon.'

'Yeah sorry Nicky. You go out Spain on the Costa Gangsta. You look up all the English cars get their numbers. Then you bell back home some insurance geezer. Geezer looks after all the companies. Repo man. Checks the motor's paid up or what.'

'And?'

'And most of 'em smell. Most of 'em doshed one payment then never again. Some old bird retiring up Spain, no point payin' up on the new motor eh? So she makes a payment then puts the Renault on the flymo, nip over the water.'

'And?'

'And the agent sends you the spare keys and some papers and you put them keys in the door then you drive the fucker away right sharp early in the morning before they wake up.'

'Back England?'

'Back England. All legit and you get a tenper.'

'Jesus. And all you got to avoid is some gangster likes his nice new Merc, didn't reckon you ought to have it away.'

'Best pick on the old biddies. More dosh on the Merc only more agg in the bargain.'

'Get upset.'

'Get very upset. You got to drive hasty.'

'Dean,' I went, 'you steppin' up the world man.'

'Tryin'. You want a trip?'

'Very busy Dean. Geezers keep wanting me to hit geezers.'

'My advice turn it down Nicky. Plenty dosh you get legit these days like I say. No need killing geezers.'

'Right.'

He got another coffee.

'You do fancy a trip,' he went, 'we do the duty free on the way back. Or we go down Calais on a daily on account of you speak Froggie.'

'You on the duties an' all Dean?'

'Serious man. Only you forget what you heard on wine and spirit and that. Fill up the motor on lager and snout. 20p in the supermarkets up Calais that lager. Retail it round the offies 40p. Five hundred cans and you made a oner. Only you make the real dosh on the snout. Tell you Nicky you can't lose. Half ounce Old Holborn they give it away Calais, retail it door to door back home £1.50. Come Christmas you got a Jeep and your jewellery and some blonde bit out of Brentwood.'

'And all legit.'

'Yeah . . . well close to legit Nicky, close to. Heard you ain't supposed to retail duty free, just a rumour.'

'Seems like you're makin' it Dean. Pay for that stripe down your coat.'

'You ain't wrong Nicky you ain't wrong.'

★ ★ ★

Then two geezers came round the corner by the market.

I just left Dean and went up the stall for a few T-shirts and that. Got my clothing grant off the Social on account of coming out of nick, reckoned it was time for a splash. Stall on the market retailed T-shirts exactly the same as the originals. Same cloth, design, dyes, name it. Original manufacturers never spot the difference. Only there was a difference, these ones came out a quiet shed on the back of Leyton industrial estate and you got them for a quarter of the original.

So I was after the T-shirts and maybe socks and underwear. Be pretty underneath. So I came round the corner by the library and these two geezers came round the other corner off the High St. Stood in my way.

One of them got a Food Giant carrier out of Selborne Walk. Clever disguise eh. Two geezers about six foot four and matching, one of them swinging a lump of wood, both of them white about thirty wearing leathers and they got a carrier for camouflage. Maybe he planned putting it over his bonce.

I turned round. There were two other geezers behind. Just behind.

Shit. I already knew I upset someone. Never knew how I did it but no matter, I upset someone. Now they sent their physicals to turn round and say they were very cross.

Oh fuck.

Fifty witnesses around. They never meant a murder. On the other hand they meant plenty to see it, give out the warning. They meant nastiness, they never planned a shopping trip with me up Food Giant.

'Morning fellers,' I went.

'Fuck off,' they all went together.

'You collecting for Oxfam?' I went. 'I reckon I just gave. Bit pushed for time now lads talk it over next week.'

There was a whack like terrible down the bottom of my back from behind. Christ it had to be a bat. I gasped out and staggered. Then a geezer in front whacked me in the neck. I went down, tried to get up.

They whacked me in the gut. I knew the next, put my mitt up. The bat crisped my fingers against my skull. I went right down, rolled away fast choking. Got on my knees then the boots came in the back. Rolled again. Out of the distance people were shouting. It couldn't last, just had to save the damage now, save the bonce. I covered up, took a kicking. Then it was gone.

Only so was I. They got me one boot on the bonce I reckoned had to crack my skull open. Thank fuck I'm out of it I thought I'm sleeping here. And I was.

In a manner of speaking I woke up after a couple of minutes. There were people. I never spoke. Felt something coming out my gob, maybe puke maybe blood maybe just dribble. Someone went 'Leave him don't turn him over'. It was the Bill. Then I was out of it again a moment, then came back on a shafting pain in the brain, never felt the rest of the body. It was splitting. There were stars, fuck me there were moons suns planets fucking neon shotguns playing inside there. There was a funny noise and it was me moaning.

There was an ambulance and they carted me away. Lifted me gentle on the stretcher still never turning me. Started the siren.

Always before I clocked the siren it was the pigs coming, made a change the ambulance going the other way. They took me up Whipps Cross and wheeled me in. Got priority alarm emergency whatever, meant I got seen less than five hours. Gradual, gradual feeling came back in the body. It hurt. Hurt round the back, the neck, the gut, the ribs and it hurt like fuck in the head.

Maybe they never meant a murder, maybe they meant a message off fifty witnesses spreading it round. Only maybe they made a mistake, totalled me by accident.

And what was the message?

I lay there quiet except the moaning.

They cut all my clothes away. Good job I never got the new ones yet, Social never would write another giro. They scanned and X-rayed and injected and patched, all the while me moaning when I wasn't sleeping and sleeping when I wasn't moaning. They patched the antiseptic and gauzes and bandages and plasters the collection. And then Jesus all of a sudden it felt so good it had to be morphine up one of the needles. I was out of it far away. They wheeled me off then and maybe they were wheeling me up heaven.

Then would you believe, last thing I clocked before I went sleeping about a year, would you believe I was in the next bed up Rameez.

* * *

I never believed it. Far away in dreamland I clocked Mum and Sharon and Kelly and little Danny and Slip. They all got baseball bats on the beach in Jamaica. Then they clocked me too and decided on whacking me up. Then there was George the warrant and Dean Longmore and they whacked me up too. Then there was Rameez all scarred and cackling and touching up the nurses. Then there were nurses. They were standing there whacking me, and when they never whacked me they reckoned I wanted another drip and a syringe.

'Nicky,' went one of them leaning over. 'Are you awake?'

'Jesus I can see up your tits,' I went. You were allowed saying things like that on account of the morphine.

Least I reckoned you were. She reckoned different. 'And you can shut your gob,' she went, 'or I'll put you back out again.'

'Sorry miss,' I went, 'it's them drugs makes you hallucinate.'

'Yeah and tell that to the marines.' Reckoned she'd been clocking too many old

Doris Day videos only best not put that in just now.

'Fuck me,' I went instead when she moved my bonce. 'Jesus H Christ that hurts.' And it did too. Pain went round shooting at me from the inside. Then she moved my body up and I reckoned maybe she stabbed me. 'YAH!' I went.

'Be brave,' she went.

'Be brave,' went Rameez cackling.

'Fuck off Rameez, excuse me miss,' I went. 'Jesus that hurt all over.'

'There, you're fixed now, you can have breakfast and you've got all your friends here.'

Eh? The fuck I got all my friends there?

Rameez was busting himself likely to come out his stitches, seemed it made a great improvement in his condition clocking me in pain.

'What happen?' I turned round and said slow and quiet.

'Look the other side Nicky,' he goes.

I turned over, only took about two weeks. Lying there the next bed asleep or unconscious was Dean Longmore.

'What the fuck?' I went.

The other side was curtained off. 'And who in there?' I went.

'Only George the warrant,' goes Rameez.

'George the warrant! What the fuck happened?' Then I had to lay back two minutes till all the pains stopped again. 'George the warrant?'

'Sure as you lay there Nicky. Dean Longmore and George the warrant.'

'What happen?'

'Only knows Nicky, only knows. Both of them got hurt a bit bad. You have to wait and ask them when they come round. Only George got his minders with him you understand. He doesn't know that yet on account of he never woke up, but he got his monkeys guarding him.'

'When they all come in?'

'Few hours after you Nicky. George got whacked about, bit like you. Dean got held and sliced on a Stanley knife, other side from where you are. Gave him a kicking too. I reckon he's sleeping out of shock you know, he ain't hurt serious bad.'

'Jesus.' I lay there and did some thinking. That hurt so I just lay there. Lay there while they took away the breakfast I never ate, lay there while they gave me regular poppers and clocked me every thirty minutes. Everything hurt when the morphine faded.

We needed some serious talking here. Only problem was in two days we never all woke up the same time for some talking. Dean came round then he went off again. George was beat up bad. All his years on warrants he never had a finger laid on him, then he got mixed up in this business we all got mixed up in whatever it was without asking, and he was beat up bad, know what I mean. When we all got conscious the same time we needed some serious talking.

★　★　★

Mum came up visiting. Made a change from visiting in prison, now she could clock her boy up the war zone. Never changed her attitude though.

'Jesus Nicky what you been bleedin' up to now you never learn do you only now I spose you'll bring on one of my migraines you bleedin' little bleeder you never think about your poor old mum or what?'

'Leave it out Mum there's geezers hear every bit you say.' I talked weak as I could playing on the sympathy, only I was wasting my time trying that on my mum.

'Geezers! I should think there's geezers! What you want's a few less geezers what are all villains every one of them. Scuse me Rameez that don't include you I know you're a good boy very good to your mum and dad and that. And you Dean you're not a bad lad underneath it all. And you Mr Marshall don't mean you of course.' Dean and George were still sleeping, never made any difference she sprayed it all round. 'What you need Nicky's a good slapping you ask me knock some sense into you.' Then she reckoned that was just what I got so she started blubbing, drank the tea she brought up out of the canteen, blubbed into it watered it down. All got very embarrassing. I went back to sleep.

Then Sharon came up and brought me some draw, went nicely with the morphine for easing the pain. She lit it up when George was still unconscious and his minders were out having a smoke. They came back sniffing only they never cared, might be on prescription.

Then Noreen came up after work.

Sat and stared at me half an hour or more. Never turned round and said a lot. Stroked my fingers nearly made me blub myself. 'Nicky you've got to give up crime,' she goes eventually.

'Noreen!' I goes. 'Noreen that ain't fair!' My condition I couldn't even raise my tones. 'Noreen I went down the market buy a T-shirt! I only just had a cup of coffee with that Dean there . . . '

'Probably planning some crime,' she turned round and said.

'Dean you hear that? Dean wake up and give evidence here geezer!' Dean never woke up. 'Noreen you gave me the message that night, no crimes and get the test' — sudden I remembered half the ward was earwigging, fuck it — 'so you reckon I went out that morning beat myself up committing some crime. Be fair Noreen I mean do me a favour know what I mean?' I wanted to cry.

'Mm,' she went thinking. Still stroking my fingers. 'Mm, maybe I'll have to consider giving you the benefit of the doubt Nicky, eh?'

Doubt? What doubt was that then? Still, never argue with a bird was my motto, never win. Birds knew best never argue, all you got was serious grief in your ears and they never admit you were right even when you were right.

Then all my mates came up, most the same ones got me the gaff and there I was not kipping in it. Ricky Hurlock Noreen's brother and Elvis Littlejohn looking cool and Wayne Sapsford took time out from nicking motors and Sherry McAllister and Paulette James and Shelley Rosario and Javed Khan. Aftab Malik and Afzal Mohammed came up visiting Rameez, wished me howdy. Half my mates visited Dean the same time when he was awake. About the same half gave George's minders palpitations, reckoned they ought to be arresting them for something, never knew what. Paulette was straight though, did that athletics for England now. Ricky was straight, and Elvis. Javed only slightly curved. The rest, well.

They brought flowers. Jesus. Chocolates and bananas. They all reckoned they paid for them, only half of them were telling porkies.

Three days then I went in and out of sleep, hurting and clocking my mates and eating bananas, only someone had to peel them for me. I never liked this, never liked this at all. I wanted that bit of blue sky and my own cup of tea and waking up in freedom. I never wanted this pain and waking up clocking a load of uniforms again.

One thing we needed that talking for was to try and make sure they never caught up with us again, whatever the fuck they were on about. Least important was what they wanted, most important was getting the fuck out of the road.

★   ★   ★

George woke up a bit eventually.

'Morning George,' I went cheery, make him feel at home.

'Jesus,' he went, 'it's a nightmare.'

'Happy to clock me innit George? How you doing old mate you want me to change your drip or something?'

'Morning George,' went Dean, walking round nicely now, due for release next day with his scar went from his lughole to his waist, bit of a big one.

'I knew it,' went George. 'It's a nightmare. Or I'm dead.'

'Hey,' went the nurse with the tits, name of Charlene, 'you leave that man alone you little horrors do you hear, before I do something to you that makes you need another brain scan, you got that?'

'All right miss all right,' I goes, 'only we're old friends you understand, on account of him being my warrant officer and that.'

'Where's his bodyguard?'

'They went out for a smoke miss left him to us knew he was safe in our hands.'

'Mr Marshall are you all right?'

'Except I got the worst beating of my life and then I woke up next door to Walthamstow's two leading yobbos, yes I guess I'm all right nurse, thank you.'

'What you got then George?' I went. 'How many bits fell off and is the chassis still in one piece?'

'God give me patience. If you really want to know they tell me I broke four ribs and one collar bone and two fingers and an ankle. They seem to think the old head's going to make it, God knows how. Anyway, what the hell are you doing here Nicky, you and Dean in those pyjamas?'

'We all got whacked George, and whacked hard. First Rameez then me and Dean, now you.'

He went all quiet. A long time he went all quiet, seemed like he nodded off again.

Then he opened up again and went 'Look Nicky we got to talk. Cut out all the crap and we talk seriously, us on the one side and you little bastards on the other.'

'Ain't we on the same side George?'

'Hah. Someone seems to think so. It seems like as soon as anyone meets you Nicky they get sorted out bad, whichever side of the law they're on. What did you do since you came out? No, never mind. Someone thinks they've got an interest in keeping you out of it, you and all your mates. We got to talk.'

'Just what I turned round and said George, we got to talk.'

'So first you get on the line and get TT in. I want to know what's going on and he needs to hear it. Tell him I want him here.'

'You got his number George?'

'Do me a favour Nicky and try not to wise-arse me just this one time all right?

Otherwise I might arrest you if I can ever get out of bed. You know the number of Chingford nick the same as I do. Just ask for CID then ask for TT.'

So I did.

★ ★ ★

TT arrived on the scene the same time as Sharon and Jimmy Foley.

'All right Nicky?' went Sharon. 'You all right now, hold a conversation?'

'All right George?' went TT. 'I heard you came round, I was waiting till you were conscious before I visited.'

'All right Mr Marshall?' went Jimmy. 'How you doin' you look pretty fuckin' bad, mind my saying so.'

'Hello Jimmy, yeah, pretty poor.'

'All right Dean?'

'All right Jimmy?'

'These minders here for you Dean or you Nicky? Which one got protection for being a supergrass then?'

'They protecting George the warrant,' I goes.

'Oh. Who they protecting him from?'

'They ain't sure, only being as it's overtime they don't give a fuck.'

'Fair enough. So how you doin' Nicky?'

'Hard.'

'You know what the fuck's goin' down round the borough?'

'Nor me nor the pigs nor even Rameez. All seem to reckon it's down to me, hear what I'm saying? Fuck knows. Go down the market buy a T-shirt, next you know you're taking brain scans and can't use your fingers.'

'Cramp your style eh?'

George was sitting up now, eating real food like lettuce leaves and bananas. He clocked us all sitting there. You couldn't hardly say he clocked us like he loved us, on the other hand it was the first time he did more than moan gently when he talked. We were his business George, he'd been taking us to court on the old fines since we were nippers, knew all our families even came to the funerals. George felt familiar with us all round.

'TT,' he went, 'we've got to do some talking here with this lot, see if we can start finding out what this is all about.'

'Talk with this lot?' went TT, looking round me and Dean and Rameez and Sharon and Jimmy like we were catching.

'Talk with him?' went Rameez and Dean and Jimmy. 'Fuckin' CID ain't he?' They all talked to CID maybe once in their lives, before they found out it only got them shafted up court. No talk no more.

'Forget what he is,' went George.

'Oh yeah,' they went.

'And TT,' went George, 'you forget what you hear in the next half hour.'

'Oh yeah,' went TT.

'Jesus,' goes George. 'Boys, and you Sharon, you got to come clean. Well, cleanish. Otherwise someone's going to get killed before we get this sorted out. TT, there's got to be no charges, all right?'

They all shut it. Anyway no-one argued.

'Right then. There's one thing I want to know to give us a better picture. We know everyone in these beds met up with something hard. Do we know if anyone else got hit or threatened, and do they know you Nicky?'

Rely on Jimmy Foley not to hold it.

'I got the warning too Nicky,' he turned round and said.

'The fuck you did. Straight up Jimmy?'

'Was just minding my business retailing a few videos round Highams Park. You reckon Darren Boardman got a copier, made a few copies of *Clockwork Orange* they made illegal. And a few others and that.'

'Good dosh on that game I heard.'

'Big pennies in videos Nicky. Retail them a fiver each round the doors, big pennies.'

'So?'

'So there I was in this gaff dealing a

*Terminator* or two and what did I hear outside?'

'Dunno Jimmy, what did you hear outside?'

'Only my motor getting shot up is all.'

'Jesus.'

'Windscreen rear window tyres the packet.'

'No accident then. No chance they hit your motor by accident aiming some other geezer.'

'No accident. Thorough shoot-up. I had to walk home.'

'Got to be tough.'

'Even more sad I only just lifted the motor. Family motor Volvo out of north Chingford, made me look like a family.'

'Volvo got shot up? Got to be a first. Geezers running Volvos ain't geezers get shot up eh?'

'You remember how I got shot once before Nicky on account of how I was drinking a pint of Guinness with you, know what I'm saying?'

'Know what you're saying.'

'Then you look all the geezers in here got shafted on account of they knew you. Then your Sharon got warned.'

'SHARON!'

'Yeah?' she went.

'Jesus you got warned Sharon?'

'Oh yeah that only I took no notice. Fuck 'em I say.'

'What they reckon?'

'Two girls visiting by Leonie's who does my hair. They went as how geezers kept on what they were doing and I could get hurt.'

'What girls? Where they from?'

'Dunno. Leonie reckoned they just called in, never saw them before and that. She went how they had to know I was coming there.'

'Jesus.' Anyone went for our Sharon and I made it my personal business to give them serious grief. 'They say what people got to stop doing what?'

'Nah. For real Nicky I reckon they only passed on a message, didn't know diddly themselves. Fuck 'em I say. Someone got an attitude, so they got an attitude. Price of peas is still the same.'

'Still the same,' went Jimmy, should have been a budgie. 'Fuck 'em I say.'

Everyone was running on, like as if the Bill were never there. Then realised that TT was petting the serious fidgets here, wanting to arrest Jimmy and Sharon and me and maybe the ward sister in the bargain, not sure what for only sure he could pin something on. Then he calmed down remembered he sort of promised.

Rameez put his penny in then, let us know he was a godfather in some streets even if he never cut it up Whipps Cross. He went wise.

'It seems to me here,' he went, 'like there ain't half a misunderstanding round some quarters about that rehabilitation you got Nicky, how you paid your debt to society. Ain't that right Mr Marshall, you get sent away then you paid your debt to society and they give you that rehabilitation to come out with? Your case Nicky you pays your debts then you comes out waiting for that rehabilitation, only it never arrives and instead you gets whacked. Then they whacks all your buddies innit? No honour in these geezers Nicky. No good man. Maybe I have to take retribution when I get out, least when I get out and can walk and see. No good at all. Like when you thieved three quarters a gallon unleaded fuel off me Nicky, I let you keep that rehabilitation, I ain't taking my debt out now four years later, know what I mean?'

Jesus. Four years was never enough time for Rameez forgetting how I lifted his day-old Audi one time by accident. Forty years might be half way enough. Might have forgotten when he'd been brown bread twenty years. Till then I lived in fear.

We sat there doing a lot of that thinking. Agreed when we all got out we'd do some serious listening in the bargain. Me, I reckoned this was never all on my account.

Couldn't put my finger on where it started

yet, only it had to be somewhere else.

Not only I never wanted this, it seemed like I never wanted to be in Walthamstow for a while now. I planned on getting away. Maybe go back up Wandsworth and have a few words with that Slip.

# 6

I sat down the canteen up Whipps Cross
when they discharged me. Gazed in a cup of
coffee maybe find the answers. I sat up a
corner and decided on starting up fresh,
pretend the last week never happened.

I got Jimmy Foley on the mobile that
Sharon brought up before I got out.

'Jimmy,' I went.

'Jimmy,' he went.

'Fuck me Jimmy,' I went, 'you're Jimmy
innit, this here's Nicky.'

'Yo Nicky,' he went. Better, that was better.

'I got released from the hospital Jimmy.'

'Out of hospital Nicky.'

'I'm in that canteen right now. What you
doing later?'

'Later?'

'What you doing later?'

'Driving around later.'

'What you doing now?'

'Driving around.'

'You want to pick me up about six?'

'About six?'

'About six. My place.'

'Your place.'

'You want that Jimmy?'

'No problem know what I mean?'

'See you later then Jimmy.'

'Later Nicky.'

I leaned back and finished my tea then and reckoned what to do next.

When I was in the nick there were four things I was desiring over the last few months. Apart from the obvious, drinking and fucking. Four things made me feel sweet. Four things you never put a real price on and I told my cellmate Slip about near release date. When I came out they all got postponed by events. Now I reckoned on doing them all straight off, that day.

So I walked out that hospital very very slow. Then even slower I walked down that Whipps Cross Rd like an old disabled geezer, till I got there, bruised and battered but I got there. Wanstead Flats, miles and miles of grass in the open air.

Few kites, few model planes. I found a nice quiet spot on that fucking grass, out in the middle of nowhere. Then I lay down on that grass and stared up at that sky.

Totalled by now, cream crackered head to toe, I stared, snoozed, nodded off. It was lovely. I was laying on the grass in the sun and snoozing. It was cool. It was ace. That was number one out of four.

Till all of a sudden it went very strange.
'MOOO!' it went.

I forgot they let the fucking cows all over the flats all summer. And the cows they got very fucking tame. So tame it seemed they came and licked your fucking chops for you. And this one decided to lick me all over my poor bleeding face, top to bottom.

Once I recovered and stopped cackling I felt a lot better, broke the ice. I got up all ready for my next treat.

The launderette.

Never had any clothes wanted washing. Mum went round my gaff and took care of all that when I was up Whipps Cross. Never mind, took a paper and just mellowed out there for an hour. I loved that launderette, just loved clocking those clothes spinning round there.

That was number two.

I went home to wait for number three now, for when Jimmy picked me up about six.

'Nicky how you doin'?' he went. 'You getting better yet or what?'

'Getting better I reckon Jimmy slowly,' I went. 'You got a motor out there, want to do me a favour?'

'Nicky, I not only got a motor, I got my own motor what's insured.'

'Insured? Insured to you?'

'Someone near me Nicky. Insured to me costs around a million quid. Insured on my mum.'

'Christ. So why is it you never took them wheels up Wandsworth that time you lifted one?'

'Not smart enough Nicky. You got to keep up appearances innit? Not smart enough go across London in an old Metro, know what I mean?'

True, you got to admit it. Seen outside Wandsworth in a Metro, never live it down.

'Jimmy, you want to take that Metro in the car wash tonight?'

'Washed it yesterday Nicky. Go up the car wash though you want, fucking give it another one eh?'

'I pay the dosh for it Jimmy. Just want to sit in there a while and let it wash over.'

'Fair enough Nicky. Fair do's. We just sit there in it.'

So we went down that car wash on Selborne Rd. I doshed. It was the super de luxe extra fucking mama and papa of all carwashes, zipped you away. It was high class, it was genial. Four years in the nick I wanted to be in that car wash clocking those brushes going backwards and forwards.

That was number three.

'Now only one thing left I want Jimmy is a

fucking great strong and fiery Indian curry. Be in heaven then. You want a fucking great Indian curry Jimmy?'

'Fucking great curry Nicky, say no more.'

So we went out that car wash down the only place to get a proper legit curry and so cheap they almost paid you for eating it, Green St down East Ham. Only problem down Green St was sometimes a bit difficult getting a meal on account of how no-one spoke English. Still, you always got a meal in the end even when it was never quite what you expected.

So we got down there in some café and negotiated a few things I never even heard of, maybe they invented them since I went away. Anyhow it was fucking hot and it was fucking tasty.

Now I got all four in one day, and I felt a whole lot better for it.

⋆   ⋆   ⋆

'Nicky what you want next?' Jimmy went over the ice cream.

'Well Jimmy . . . ' I never knew how to put this, felt kind of stupid, preferred talking up birds over soft stuff not Jimmy Foley. 'Well Jimmy . . . I was thinking of going straight you reckon.'

He sat there and goggled at me.

'Nicky . . . You ain't well. That hospital you caught something in the brain there.'

'Thinking of going straight Jimmy.'

'Nicky . . . You ain't well geezer. You got release fever, you ain't thinking yet you got to get rehabilitated.'

'That Noreen gave me the message.'

'Noreen . . . Noreen Hurlock? Nicky you ain't knockin' off Noreen Hurlock? Jesus Nicky, only the best bit of . . . scuse me Nicky she ain't only the tastiest looking bird in town, she . . . Jesus Nicky I see what you're meaning mate I got to see your angle here. Noreen Hurlock reckons you got to go straight for her?'

'Yeah. The size of it.'

'Phew.' Jimmy wiped his forehead. 'Jesus Nicky you got it tough man. Noreen Hurlock, what can I say?'

'What it is, see, she reckons I want to poke her I got to go straight.'

He took this in. 'Wow Nicky, tough choice eh, tough choice,' he went. 'Got to be ultimate. She even got a job up West and you heard she got them cheap flight tickets Nicky?'

'Yeah I heard.'

'So what you decided?'

'Tell you the truth Jimmy I don't know what I want.'

'You want another curry Nicky after that ice cream?'

'And then get another curry tomorrow night.'

'Now you're talking. Makes sense Nicky get that curry in, only first you got to get the dosh for the curry eh, it don't come out of no giro innit?'

'That Noreen goes to work every day Jimmy. What you think I'm going to do while she's out at work? Ain't no jobs round Walthamstow.'

Jimmy stared me out over the table and whistled. 'Jesus Nicky you got a problem,' he went. 'You ain't got release fever you got woman fever, much more serious, warp your mind.'

I was confused. No danger I was confused.

'What the fuck you gonna do?' Jimmy went.

⋆ ⋆ ⋆

I went up West for the test.

Got the tube from Walthamstow Central up Euston then walked. Found the road and then the clinic. Stood across the street outside staring at it and sweating.

Kind of geezers went in there? Diseased geezers? Touch me up geezers? Want to share

114

a needle in the back room?

Do what you got to do.

I went over the street and straight in the main door without stopping. Inside were two signs, one men's clinic and one some long word clinic. Noreen told me she booked me in the men's clinic, good start anyway get a reservation.

I went in the door. Christ there were geezers all round. They seemed like they were all reading newspapers till I came in the door, then they all looked up together.

'I came for the test!' I went in the middle of the floor.

I meant to say it when I got up the desk only it sort of jumped out earlier than it was supposed to. No-one collapsed or asked for a sedative though. They all started reading their newspapers again.

'Oh hello,' went the lady behind the desk, 'can I help you, have you got an appointment?'

'Yeah my bird like booked me in,' I went. 'Nicky Burkett and that.' Wanted them to know I got a bird not like some of them eh.

'Oh yes, Mr Burkett, here it is. Is this your first time here?'

Christ yes.

'Christ yes,' I went.

'Well, I'll just ask you to fill in this form

then if you could please.'

I went and sat down next some geezer, seemed normal never touched me up. Filled in the form. Glanced crafty round the room. There were some geezers nervous like me, you could clock them sweating. Others acted like they were old lags, going 'Hi there' to the nurses and docs they knew. I was wondering who got the lurgy and who never, couldn't tell by looking.

I gave the form back and the lady smiled. 'Please take a seat then,' she went, 'and one of the doctors will see you shortly.'

Just like that.

I tried reading the paper only found I was reading it upside down. I tried thinking about the lady's tits only I couldn't concentrate. Sooner wait for a punch-up on association down Wandsworth than this.

'Mr Burkett!' went the voice.

'ME!' I went, took me by surprise. Then the doc turned round and went in an office and I followed him.

'Hello,' he went smiling, smart geezer snappy dresser. 'Do sit down please Mr Burkett, what can I do for you?'

'I came for the test mister,' I went.

'What sort of test would you like? We can do them all here you see. Hepatitis A, Hep — '

'Aids test,' I went. 'Me bird booked me in for the Aids test Doc.'

'Ah yes, the HIV test, that's fine.'

'Fine.'

'That will be no problem at all. Oh, by the way, and just as a bonus we also do a syphilis test at the same time, it's routine you know.'

'Syphilis!'

'Yes, it's all one sample but we do two tests on it you see, it's very convenient.'

'Syphilis! Doc I don't mind so much I got Aids but syphilis no I ain't having none of that Doc straight up.'

'It's mere routine Mr Burkett, I'm sure you haven't got it, but it's always better to be on the safe side and you don't have to do anything you see.'

I thought on it. Got to go ahead now I got here or face that Noreen.

'Go on then Doc,' I goes.

'Thank you very much Now, first I must ask you a few questions, is that all right?'

'Yeah, sweet, Doc, go right ahead ask them questions.'

'Thank you. When did you last have sex?'

Jesus.

'Well,' I goes, 'now you're talking Doc.' Proper embarrassing. 'Half the trouble right now I ain't had it, it got to be last home leave that Kelly gave it me only now she don't want

117

to know, would you credit it. Only that Noreen she's like my new bit of stuff, you got to know she's fucking brilliant, excuse me Doc, only she reckons I got to get the test first.'

'I see . . . So when do you think your last home leave was, approximately?'

'Got to be two months Doc, got to be if it's a day.'

'Right. Who was this with?'

'That Kelly I told you about.'

'I see. And, now, is that Kelly a man or a woman?'

I had to cackle. Reckoned I'd ask her the same question next time I clocked her, tell her the clinic wanted to know. 'Got to be a woman last time I did it with her,' I went.

'Of course. Would you like a cup of tea Mr Burkett?'

'Now you're talking Doc, could murder a cup of tea honest. Got to tell you I'm right nervous you reckon.'

'Well, that's only natural. Now I'll just ask you a few more questions if I may. What sort of sex was this last time, was it casual or in a relationship or what was it?'

'Pretty casual Doc, seemed like she never bothered tell you the truth. When I think back on what she was like them early days . . . '

'Yes I'm sure. Was it protected or unprotected sex?'

'Unprotected I reckon.'

'Thank you. Now have you been ill at all? Any weight loss, any night sweats? No?'

Wanted to tell him there wasn't a thing wrong with me only I just got to take the test was all. 'No,' I went.

'Have you had any high risk contacts as far as you know? Do you inject drugs? Have you had many relationships?'

'No to the first Doc. Unfortunately no to the second the last few years.'

'I see. Now, before I take this blood, or rather ask the nurse to take this blood, would you like to see a counsellor? You have thought carefully about exactly why you want to have the HIV test?'

He was a good geezer the doc. The nurse was a good geezer. The lady in reception was a good geezer. I thanked them every one of them and I got the test and they told me to come back in a couple of weeks. Then I fucked off out of there sweating like a policeman and shaking like a leaf. I got the fear. I went out and got five pints of lager, then I calmed down enough to go home.

# 7

'Slip,' I went, 'so how do I get to that Jamaica then eh?'

'Hah!' he turned round and said. 'Hah! Knew you'd come over Nicky knew you'd got to man.'

'Shut the fuck up Slip and just give me the news how I get there eh? There a plane or what?'

'Course there's a fuckin' plane brother, *brmm brmm* like a motor you dig? You think we people travel by raft? Wings and a tail that have too, only it ain't never a bird.'

'Yeah yeah. So where do I catch this machine? Heathrow?'

'First you got to get a ticket Nicky.'

'Ticket? I never got no ticket I went up France.'

'Only you went up France on a boat innit? Then you prob'ly got a ticket before they let you on. Get on a plane you got to purchase a ticket just the same, only you required to obtain it in advance.'

'Shit.'

He sipped his rosie and gnawed on his biscuit. 'So you want me to inform you how you get a ticket my brother Nicky Burkett?'

'Do that. Then shut the fuck up.'

'First you purchase one copy of *The Voice*. Then you bell all the merchants advertise flights to Jamaica. Then you compare prices and you check on the dates are convenient. Then you decide you go whenever is cheapest and fuck the dates. Then you go next week is always the cheapest of all. Then you exchange the required sum of spending money for one of their best tick-ets.'

'Jesus. Pretty fuckin' complicated ain't there a shop I can just go down?'

'That the way you got to do it like I just described. Yes there is a shop, in fact there is two shops, one called BWIA and one just called BA. And it cost you a song and there just as good a chance the thing done crash anyway. So you being a person of skill and initiative, and you being a person of no serious dosh, you got to do the work on the markets.'

'So I does the deal and then I goes down and pays?'

'Nah. Ain't nobody goes down and pays like buying a chocolate bar. You pays by credit card Nicky Burkett.'

'Credit card? Whose credit card? I got to go thieving in the bargain?'

'Jesus Nicky Burkett ain't you got your own credit card? Ain't no call to go thieving. You

121

surely got a credit card?'

'Had a whole fistful one time Slip only never one like personal. You got to be working get a credit card. They ain't brought work round Walthamstow yet.'

'Oh my Gawd this going to be complicated. So maybe you got to pay paper after all. You got paper?'

'Get a giro Friday.'

'Giro get you on that big bird far as Slough. You still got real paper stashed away like you said?'

'Enough.'

'Say no more. So that get you there and back, then we think about you living cheap when you get out there. Maybe you go to visit by my grannie when you go Jamaica.'

'Grannie.'

'She feed you. Go there every two days, I tell you she meals last you two days. Tell her news of her boy that me. She real nice lady. She poor but she real nice and I loves her. Miz Lucy. She feed you big.'

'Sure I visit her. You got any rich relations too?'

'I got a uncle up country runs a bar. Keep you drunk.'

'Do my best.'

'We come back to that later. First we talk business.'

I went up the WVS for more of that tea and Twix. Hurt even moving only I never brought company this time. So we sat down again and we sipped and we chewed and we looked serious. This was it, this was the moves.

'Nicky,' he went.

'Slip,' I turned round and said.

'Nicky,' he turned round and said, 'now I tell you the business in detail. Import export the whole deal.'

'You got me.' I sipped the tea serious.

'Nicky, first you know I say how you export them deckchairs up Jamaica?'

'I knows.'

'Well, on this trip you got to do two things straight off. Like business research.'

'Business research.'

'First you got to check out the market for deckchairs, see if they got them loungers. See the guvnors run them hotels. Check out the public beaches too see if they want them deckchairs to hire out. Talk to the man, you dig?'

'Dig.'

'Then second you got to check out what you bring back, what you bring back from Jamaica. Import export innit?'

'Jamaica only got one export right?'

'No Nicky where you wrong man. Stuck in the ganja groove you is. OK so I slipped up there one bit. Only Jamaica got plenty export. Bauxite for beginnings.'

'You want me export bauxite?'

'Never get it in your suitcase man. You hear what is this bauxite?'

'Nope.'

'Never you mind. Let's talk about that coffee I mentioned.'

'Coffee? You for real?'

'Jamaican Blue Mountain coffee. Only the best coffee in the world is all.'

'What about Nescaff?'

'Jesus Nicky. There are times you try my patience man. Talkin' real coffee here. And the realest of the real. Japanese they pay so many yen for that coffee you never get it in your piggy bank. Americans drink it weak as piss only way they can afford it. Brits never drink it at all, obvious reasons. There ain't a lot of it and it got to come from the right place for to be Blue Mountain coffee, up the Blue Mountains in the cloud, you dig? It top prices only and we got to get on it.'

'How we do that?' Couldn't help but notice it was we, only it was me going across the water.

'Well let me give you a lesson about coffee bro'. I got all this off my grannie when I was up there. She brother a farmer. You listen up good?'

'Listen.'

'There is a big coffee factory see. They roast them beans, they grind them up, they package them, they do the business. Now there's big coffee farmers they maybe never go through the factory they got them own operations. They roast them beans then they grind them up or they leave them whole, then they sell independent up some international dealer. They Japs they even bought a factory themselves. So them big farmers they either deal themselves direct or they put a little through the factory and the Board, you dig? We no messing with them.'

'Dig. No messing.'

'Only then there's the little farmers.'

'They pygmies?'

'Shut the fuck up Nicky, you ain't got no sense of humour. They little farmers they got maybe two three acres. They roast a few beans themselves sell up the tourists. Only the rest they got to go through the factory and then they got to go through the Board. Ain't got no choice, can't sell straight up Tokyo. So they sell up the Board and they get rip off. Board sell up Tokyo four times the price.'

'Four times.'

'So you got to get up them small farmers Nicky. Get them beans, few here few there.

No even pay tourist prices, not at all. Explain you may want plenty more later. Get them real cheap cheap. Still a nice profit in it for them little farmers only not tourist profit. You take a empty suitcase out there first time. This like a reconnaissance a exploratory mission. No bother with export licence this time only try for paying your expenses you see? You bring back that suitcase full of coffee then, be surprised could even pay for your tick-et. You dig? Then we start real business. Jamaican coffee in London at a price the punter can afford!'

'And deckchairs in Jamaica!'

'Wild!' He got excited, stood up and punched the air, then he was wasted, sat back gasping in his chair. 'We be millionaires,' he went. 'Then we got a platform for setting up that deal on Senegal . . . '

'Oh yeah. Forgot about that.'

'Don't forget about that Nicky. This is a long term business plan very long term. You remember about that *modus operandi*?'

'Slipped my mind one second.'

'Well now we make plans for that *modus operandi* Nicky.'

So we got down to the plans on the details.

★   ★   ★

I took Noreen by Mrs Shillingford.

Mrs Shillingford was ninety-one. I got sent round hers a few years before on that Community Service, supposed to dig up her garden or some shit. I started on the garden got blisters. Fuckin' roll on, I thought, they're makin' joke here havin' a laugh. I went and knocked on her door.

'Scuse me Mrs Shillingford,' I turned round and said, 'only my hands hurt you get my meaning?'

'I get your meaning,' she goes. 'It is hard work isn't it? Would you like a cup of tea for your break?'

'Oo, not wrong Mrs Shillingford, not wrong.'

So we went in her house and had a cup of tea and a yack about it. And it turned out she got the arthritis, and deaf on one side and blind on the other and not very good either side. Took us a half hour each week looking for her specs. And one other thing about her. She loved to yack.

'Yes,' she went. 'It is hard work that gardening but good. I used to have a garden back home, we grew yams and plantain and green beans and breadfruit, it was hard hard work. I tell you what young man. Perhaps we can come to some arrangement. You do one hour each week on my garden. Then you can come in the house if you prefer and help me tidy up and cook. What do you have to say about that?'

'Tidy up?' I went. 'Cook Mrs Shillingford? So what happens when some geezer gets to hear, tells everyone I'm a woman?'

'So you be a man,' she goes.

'Eh?'

'You tell them it none of their blasted business.'

'Oh.' Not too sure that stopped them laughing the fuck out of me. Still, kept me out the garden. Then she taught me that cooking.

So she sat there could hardly move or see, blinked at me and the stove and the veg I brought round off the market and she told me the knockings. Not long before I made yam and sweet potato stew I reckoned was the best in Walthamstow no danger, just let anyone say different.

And dasheen and green bananas and rice and peas and eggs and beans and hot sauce, you name it. Then we ate it and she ran round the verbals on Dominica in the old days, her village and her boyfriends and the Carnival and the music out of Trinidad and Brazil even. Then more music on the swing bands, on account of how she loved geezers called Benny and Artie, or more often

128

Benjamin and Arthur to her. Then we started on her rum. I got there nine in the morning, often went home eleven at night. That Community Service flew away only I kept going.

So now I took Noreen round by Mrs Shillingford. Belled her first told her I was on the way up. Got there Saturday dinner time, took her a Caribbean takeaway off Markhouse Rd.

'Mrs Shillingford,' I yelled loud through the letter box.

'Come in Nicky dear it is open.'

Went in.

'Mrs Shillingford I brought someone, like this here's Noreen.'

'This who?'

'This Noreen.'

'Noreen you say?' She shuffled round in her chair, put her teacup away, put her teeth in, took a butcher's. 'Come round here Noreen can you find my spectacles let me get a good look at you.' We all hunted round till we found her specs then we shifted so she got Noreen in the right spot for clocking her. Then she inspected.

'Nicky,' she went, 'I do believe this is a very pretty young woman you have brought to see me. What is she doing with you?'

'Fancies me I reckon Mrs Shillingford.'

Noreen whapped me.

'And not only pretty but very smart and polite looking into the bargain. Is she clever too?'

'She reckons only don't believe everything you hear Mrs Shillingford. Just thought I'd bring her by you for a visit.'

'I heard such a lot about you Mrs Shillingford,' went Noreen.

'Hmph. So this is your young lady Nicky?'

'You could say that. Only you could say she ain't. On account of we watch a video together now and again only she never gave me a touch of the other yet, drives me mental know what I mean?'

'Nicky Burkett!' went Noreen.

'Nicky Burkett!' went Mrs Shillingford.

'Scuse me Mrs Shillingford,' I went.

'Nicky,' goes Noreen, 'there is some business between women here. Now will you please go and stand in the street a bit. Mrs Shillingford and I have got some serious talking to do I do believe.'

Mrs Shillingford cackled till it looked she'd do herself a mischief. 'Hoo,' she went, 'I believe we have got some talking to do just a little talking. Hoo Nicky, I never heard anyone speak to you like that before. My life!'

So I cackled got to. Went off and got a video and came back and took time out for

130

two or three hours. They were still yacking on their woman talk, probably all the way from shoes round grandchildren round sex round cooking same as usual. And they never even got a sore throat. I went to sleep after the video only woke up when the kettle went off, just when Noreen was booking another visit for next Saturday. She never mentioned whether I was coming or not, only booked for herself.

★ ★ ★

Then it got bad.

Sunday night I was clocking a video when the phone rang.

'Yeah.'

'Burkett?' went the voice.

The fuck was this Burkett?

'And who the fuck are you when you're at home?' I went.

'Burkett I've got news for you. You and your mates have been stepping on a few toes.' Heavy voice, heavy news.

'Yeah?' I goes. 'Clocking a fucking video mate is all the fuck I'm doing.'

'We gave you a warning before and you still took no notice. You've been up Wandsworth visiting your little mate, planning a bit of importation no doubt?'

'Shared a Mars Bar with him all right? You finished?'

'Maybe you ought to look up your girlfriend.'

Then the Voice was gone.

And of course the number was never stored when I checked it.

I sat down and turned off the video. Who the fuck was my girlfriend?

Noreen?

I was out the door and running. On the way I was dialling on the mobile. Girlfriend might still be Kelly even? Out of date only Kelly got the kid. I went running for a cab on Hoe St, before I got there reached Kelly on the mobile.

'Kelly,' I went still running, 'you all right and the kid?'

'Yeah course Nicky what's the game, why you panting, you takin' the piss?'

'You got anyone with you?'

'Yeah Barry's here and Danny, no-one else.'

'Stay indoors till you hear from me. Never answer the door, stay out of line the doors and windows, you got that?'

'Yeah I got that. Nicky what's up?'

'Fuck knows only I just got a warning. You get any agg, any agg at all, you bell 999 you got that?'

'I got that Nicky.'

'Right.' I rang off.

Then I belled Noreen's home.

No answer.

Belled it again make sure I dialled right. No answer, no answer machine.

Got to the cab office. Got a cab. Belled Ricky Hurlock Noreen's brother on his mobile. He answered.

'What?' he went.

'Ricky it's me. Noreen all right?'

'Why?'

'Ricky I just got a call, went watch out for my girlfriend. She all right?'

'Nicky we're up Whipps Cross.'

'NO!'

'Better come and see for yourself Nicky.'

'Ricky what's it? What's it man?'

'She got cut.'

'Ricky ten minutes.'

I stood outside the cab office. I walked round shaking.

Got the cab to go up Whipps Cross up Casualty and ran straight in there. Stared round never clocked them. Went up the desk and asked. Next thing I knew I got my collar felt.

'Fuck off God's sake just tell me what the fuck's happening man.' It was TT, fucking DS Holdsworth no less, got to be packing in the overtime, never get CID on duty Sunday night as a rule. 'Fucking tell me man, sort out the details later.' My stomach was going over. There was the fear in there.

'Nicky now hold it one minute. She's all right. Someone held her and cut her down the cheek. Come and sit round the corner a minute, calm down before you see her. She's in there being stitched at the minute, her family's all here.'

We went round the corner in a room, like a cubicle. I sat and shook. Knew I had to cool it. Clocked him straight up the eyeballs.

Then I went 'What you doing here you scumhead?'

'Hospital rang the station. Station knew I had an interest.'

'Interest in Noreen? You fucker, you fuckin' shitbag you . . . '

'Hang on Nicky. Won't do her any good will it? Me having an interest never got her hurt, it was more likely a connection with you I'm sorry to say. Now her brother told me what you said on the phone to him just now, so we'll talk about that afterwards, see if we can make any sense out of it. First you want to cool it, see your girlfriend, do the best you can for her. All right?'

Fucking shitbag. I went out and found Noreen's mum and dad and Ricky in the corridor. Known them all my fucking life since I went to school with Ricky. His dad used to take us to football Sunday mornings. Now I got their daughter sliced.

And they just looked at me.

Then her dad got up, slow and quiet.

'Now don't say anything Nicky just yet,' he went. 'We know it's not your fault man, Ricky told us. We know you wouldn't do anything that might harm Noreen. It's best we none of us say anything too soon.'

Her mum was crying. I went over to her and she hugged me. Fuck me I never knew anything this bad.

Then the nurse came out pulling the curtain. 'Please could you just give her two minutes,' she turns round and says, 'then you can go in. Nice and quiet, don't you upset yourselves or you'll upset her you know.'

Two minutes then we went in.

Noreen sat there on the chair a bit hunched up. She was pale and small.

She clocked round all of us.

'I got seventeen stitches,' she went.

It started by her hairline between her eye and ear. It went down the side of her cheek to her neck. It was narrow. Stanley knife job. I found out later she got held and told to be still or it got worse. They got her on the road near home, coming back off Sunday after-noon visiting.

She sat there, then she went to her mum. Then her dad. Then Ricky. Then last she came to me and she gave me a hug in the bargain.

'Noreen . . . '

'Don't say anything Nicky you don't have to, I know it isn't anything you did. I don't know what it is but I know it isn't you.'

One thing I knew. I was getting the bastard.

I heard The Voice, and some time I was going to waste him.

'They say it really won't leave much of a scar,' Noreen went.

★   ★   ★

Then that Dean Longmore dropped me up Gatwick on the Wednesday.

Dean was still sore all over his body and he got a scar healing up from neck to waist.

I was sore. I was boiling inside. I was going to kill someone.

Noreen reckoned I got to go. Bought the ticket got to go, be the same when I got back. I never wanted to go, wanted to stay behind and kill someone. I thought about her every fucking minute I was away. But I got to go. Thinking about her. Hating some geezer like I never hated.

I was running.

We cruised down Mile End and past the Tower and up Brixton.

'Dean,' I went, 'you reckon you got a problem or what?'

'What you say?'

'You reckon this lassoing kind of grabbed you by the bollocks then or what?'

'Eh?'

'You lasso this Jeep? Kind of smart innit for lassoing?'

'Jeep's lifted Nicky you got to know that eh?'

'Lifted! New model probably got a fucking tracker on it! Reckoned you were legit Dean!'

'Never take you up Gatwick in a legit motor Nicky. First off I ain't got the dosh on a new-style Jap Jeep yet. Second off it ain't got no style. Not worthy of you man.'

Jesus.

We went up Streatham Hill passing eighty and we were cruising.

*Living in a land of sweet Jamaica*
*Soon everything is gonna be all right*

We hit a hundred on the motorway. Me I was getting by on a bottle of whizz and some Es before I went out last night. Dean was getting his speedies off lassoing bleeding motors.

137

We got to Gatwick an hour early. Sign said: Gatwick.

'What happen now Dean?' I went. 'Where is it I go man?'

'You ever caught a plane before Nicky?'

'Well . . . not in a manner of speaking.'

'Me either. Best you ask a policeman I reckon.'

'Shit.'

We parked the Jeep in a car park. Neither of us used to driving in car parks either, only borrowed motors out of them. Two terminals Gatwick, meant nothing round me and Dean so one car park same difference as the other. We got my bag out the boot. Clocked a sign said Departures, reckoned that was me.

Place was full of people. Seemed best we head for Information, nice and cool, chill out.

'I came for a plane,' I went.

'You don't say.'

'You got one going?'

'More than one. How many would you like?'

'One for my man here take him home. One for me catch up Jamaica.'

'Jamaica eh? That's a long way.'

'That the truth? I heard it was other side of Brighton lady.'

She checked me out down her hooter. 'All right smartipants,' she went, 'what do you want to know before I chew you up and spit you out?'

'That the way you supposed to speak to the punters missis?'

'You aren't a regular punter sunshine. You aren't even a tourist. I can speak to you how I like and you probably wouldn't even notice. I bet you wouldn't even know how to make a complaint.'

Me and Dean we fell about laughing. She wasn't wrong.

'What you doing after all the planes left?' went Dean 'You fancy a ride round the tarmac? Few lagers up Brighton?' Let her see his scar.

'Let you play with my children maybe,' she went, 'they're about your age.'

She pointed me up for collecting my ticket then the rest of the moves, all that customs and that. Like how you got on the fucking plane. I gave her thanks, lady of niceness. And she winked. And she got good tits.

'Give her the time of day,' went Dean. 'Only she made you low life Nicky, you wouldn't never even get started.'

'True.'

Very good tits though considering she had to be thirty-five if she was a day. We cackled. Then Dean he turned round and went home.

$\star$  $\star$  $\star$

They reckoned flying you listened up some sounds and clocked the video and gobbed some wine and the meal and yacked your neighbour then you had a little snooze. Only they never told you what you did afterwards. Done all that in half an hour. I counted on sitting next some fine Jamaican piece dying for it. Instead I got me some old biddy in a hat and a Chinese geezer never spoke English.

'All right mate?' I went up the Chinese geezer.

'All right mate?' he went, seemed like the only words he knew.

'All right mate?' I went up the old biddy.

'Good morning,' she turns round and says. 'I place my faith in God that this machinery will not let me down today.'

'Got to hope he passed his City and Guilds then,' I went. 'And brought his spanner.'

Then they shut the door.

So after a bit when we were up in the sky and we finished the grub and I listened up some sounds I had me a little snooze. By now the Es were wearing off so I faded away nicely. And while I was fading I went over the last part my conversation with Slip telling me what I got to do in Jamaica. Just like it was Stratford or Leyton.

'Nicky you got to go up Mavis Bank,' he went.

'She your cousin or what?'

'Nicky you go up any of my fambly while you out there I cut it off man with a cutlass. Mavis Bank like a place. Where my grannie live.'

'Grannie.'

'And Mavis Bank where you think that is? Only in the mountains is all, where they grow that coffee?'

'Coffee.'

'So you understand how sweet it is? You go see my grannie, she give you a big meal, you take her a bottle of vodka.'

'Vodka? Reckoned they all took that rum.'

'My grannie Miz Lucy she like a tipple of that vodka. Put in her sour sop. So you go up Mavis Bank and you ask for Miz Lucy and she give you a big meal . . . '

'We did that bit, and I takes her the vodka.'

'And you takes her the vodka and you ask her where you go purchase some coffee. Blue Mountain coffee. It is expanding market . . . '

'We did that bit too.'

'Then you go up that mountain and you look up them little farmers . . . '

I snoozed and woke up and snoozed and woke up. It was fucking boring. Then the pilot came on again gave it a bit of chat.

141

'Ladies and gentlemen,' he went, 'we are now beginning our descent into Miami.'

'Miami!' I goes. 'Miami!'

'That what he say I do believe,' goes the old biddy.

'Scuse me lady,' I goes to the waitress clambering over the China geezer, 'scuse me lady you reckon this pilot took a wrong turn or what, I got a ticket here says Jamaica you hear what I'm saying? Miami!'

'Yes sir we go to Jamaica via Miami,' she goes.

'We do?'

'Yes sir.'

'Oh.' So I sits down again going sorry like. And eventually we got round Jamaica.

# 8

We got up customs.

'All right mate?' I went up the man.

He clocked me like I was a Scouser.

'Did you pack your bag yourself?' he went.

'Eh?' Funny sort of question.

'I said did you pack your bag yourself sir?'

'Course I did like.'

'And are there any firearms or similar items in it?'

No Nicky, I thought, best not start the first Caribbean war here over some piece of wit. Best stay cool not vex the man.

'No,' I goes, 'there ain't no firearms in it. Straight up mate.'

'Thank you sir. Welcome to Jamaica.'

So I went out the door and got welcomed by the rest of Jamaica. They were lined up outside. Not only they wanted to welcome me they wanted to take all my dosh. They wanted to retail me taxis and hire cars and ganja and their uncle's T-shirts and more ganja. I went off and got a Red Stripe let them settle down. Took the names of six cabbies with me case I wanted to take six cabs.

Red Stripe tasted like it always did, weak

piss only don't be telling no Jamaican that. I made it last a while then slunk out the airport while the vultures were nobbling some other geezer.

It was hotter in Jamaica.

Down the end round the quiet part of the taxi rank I pulled some cabbie sitting on his bonnet.

'Scuse me geezer only you point me out the road up some guesthouse mate I can shank to never need no cab?' I went.

He clocked me a minute. 'I beg your pardon,' he went, 'but do you speak any English because I have some trouble with German?'

'German!' I went. 'True blue mate me. Want me to run it by you again mate?'

He waited a bit. Then he went 'What is your name, young man?'

'Nicky.'

'I am called Francis. I believe you would prefer not to take a taxi is that right?'

'Correct. Never want you running out of business mate only I aren't lined you reckon and hoped you never minded pointing out like a guesthouse what I heard there's some so I never spend the dosh.'

'You know I believe you really are British are you not?'

'Walthamstow mate no danger.'

'Well well. I must introduce you to my daughter, she is a postgraduate student of English in London. I believe she would be very interested to meet you. Just for the record, incidentally, I am not a cabbie but a doctor, and I am waiting here to meet my daughter off the next plane from London. If you wouldn't mind waiting a few minutes I would be very pleased to drop you at a guesthouse. There is one on my way home.'

Oh.

Shit.

'Look mate,' I went, 'this is proper embarrassing I had you down as a cabbie sat here.'

'That is perfectly all right, taxi driving is a very honourable profession and it is true that I am sitting here on a car. This man next door after all is indeed a taxi driver.' He pointed out another geezer in the shadows and the geezer nodded. 'He is an old school friend of mine. He is called Barnyard.'

'All right mate?' I went.

'Yes man good night.'

Then this Barnyard he went something to the doc I never reckoned a word of. Then the doc went something to him and I never reckoned that either. They yacked a few minutes and I never made one word.

'Scuse me here Doc,' I went.

'Yes Nicky?'

'Scuse me only what language you were yacking in then?'

'English my friend.'

'Oh.'

'English as spoken here in Jamaica but English nevertheless. There may be a few words that we introduce ourselves.'

Reckoned it was going to be a hard week I got round Jamaica. Half of Walthamstow was Jamaica only I never earholed any Jamaican like that. Nor on the ragga neither.

'Ah, here is my daughter.' She came out of that door and they gave it all the hugs and kisses and she blubbed a bit. Then he went 'Jane I would like you to meet a young Englishman, Nicky. We have been having a very interesting time here talking about languages.'

'Please tameetcha Nicky,' she went, 'you all right then mate or what?' Then she started giggling when she clocked her old man's expression.

'Jane!' he went.

'All right Daddy don't you fret,' she went, 'that's how they talk in England you know, you have to greet them in their language or they just won't understand you now. They rub noses as well.'

'Jane . . . ' She was taking the piss here.

'You been round Walthamstow when you was up London?' I went.

'I think I've heard of it,' she went. 'Isn't it on a tube line?'

'Not just on a tube line lady, not just on a tube line it's the end of the line innit? Walthamstow Central no danger. Got five stations Walthamstow, three of them on one line, one of them Walthamstow Central.' Then I stopped on account of no-one was taking any notice, they were still hugging and that.

And you had to credit it she was a doll in the bargain that Jane. Got to be brainy it sounded like, only she was a living totty. Long straight hair, body curved and blew around, nose turned up, she reckoned all the days of the week no danger.

'You been clocking the action then Nicky?' she went. Then she howled laughing since the doc nearly got an epileptic. 'Jane my dear girl,' he went, 'is that really the language they speak where you study? Does your linguistics option take that in? I think you should not speak like that even in jest. You might easily get infected and not be able to revert to normal English.'

She winked at me then that Jane. Made two birds in one day winked at me. Only trouble was you could tell neither of them was ever going to pass a slice of the action my way if we were locked up on a desert island. No hard feelings only they got class.

They dropped me off at a guesthouse and the doc gave me their number and address case I got any problems. Seemed to reckon I was headed for a few of them.

Got to be an all right geezer the doc. I gave him the thanks and booked in.

I was in Jamaica.

*   *   *

Next morning I got the bus into Kingston. Me and about seven hundred others made the bus a bit full.

I got some very close acquaintances on that bus and made a tidy examination of the inside someone's hooter. No-one seemed fussed though so we got to the other end and I wondered if I broke any more bones.

Then it got more exciting when I came out of Kingston bus station. Round here was gun city so they reckoned.

So I put the bag over the shoulder and set off for downtown through about thirty geezers wanting me to take a ride in their motor instead. Half of them sell me a few other things in the bargain. Shook them off and headed out on the road on foot. Only it was wild.

Heard about Kingston bus station but it was never the station was the problem. Area outside got a very very big touch of how's your father, very very big touch indeed. There was more than a few lads doing a bit of ducking and diving, there was more than a few looked like they knew which way up you held a machete. Reminded me of Bosnia that sniper's alley they had on the news. Never clocked any mortars but the paper that day had a list every other weapon they used on that week's bank raids. They reckoned most of them made their first home round that bus station.

'Eh white man!'

Most of the lads never gave a problem never even gave an attitude. Only a few reckoned they owed me a calling. I walked very soft past the veg stalls along a row of shacks. Never let anyone bump into you bad policy. Never meet any geezer's big stare. Never upset geezers. Then try making out you never exist at all. I kept down low.

'Eh white man!'

Over the distance was high rise city. Half of Kingston was like Canary Wharf, the other half Hackney after the bomb. None of it was like Walthamstow. Nor even Tottenham.

Woman came up and asked where I was headed. Fuck knows, wanted to turn round and say, and I'm shitless. 'Downtown,' I went, on account of I read it somewhere. 'Well you not far,' she went, 'you go up there and turn right there. Now you get out of this area fast eh?'

'Thanks lady,' I went, then took my little tootsies off quick.

I made it. Came out of Kingston bus station and lived to tell.

Slip reckoned Papine was the starter for where I wanted. Got a coffee in a burger bar and the geezer went how to get the 14 up Half Way Tree then the 70 or 75 up Papine. 'Thanks mate,' I went.

Changed some paper in the bank over the road and the bird gave me small notes separate. 'Put the big notes away safe,' she went, 'then you just take out a few dollars for the bus fare, otherwise there are men who make thief you know.' Then I climbed up the bus, got a tour of Kingston without ever clocking a sight on account of how my bonce was up the ceiling and I never could shift an inch. Woman in charge reckoned she was a prison officer. 'Step up!' she went, like I wasn't in someone's pocket already. 'Step up!'

We all got out at Half Way Tree and I got the 75. Went past Marley's gaff. This 75 was half empty only about four hundred folks on it so I got a butcher's up Marley's. Then a bit later that was it. Papine. End of the line.

That was Kingston I just did. Never believed it. Come all this way, been Kingston, seen fuck all.

Papine was different. Big square with stalls round it. Shacks round the square like and a few shops. Kind of basic. Folk yacking. Geezers making themselves busy only no-one seemed like going anywhere. Plenty plenty noise plenty to say. Women sitting in the shade.

'Bag juice bag juice!' went the sellers. 'Box drink box drink!' Only they never seemed to mean it too strong, never fussed you one way or the other.

I got a drink and a bit of bulla cake. The lady seller pointed the bus up Mavis Bank. Bus sat there not in any hurry. Round there you waited till a bus felt like going, like when it was full or the driver did all his messages or maybe till the wind was the right way. After an hour we were off. Minibus so they only got a hundred or so on it.

We set off up that road.

In Papine you already saw the mountains. I was never used to mountains. Only mountain we got round Walthamstow was Chingford Mount. Jamaican mountains were bigger.

In the bargain there were more of them, far as the eye could clock. Then they got forest on them, and grass and scrub and more forest. I goggled. None of that up Chingford Mount. Now we were going up there in that minibus.

We set off up that road. Went straight for a bit like natural up a valley. Then that bus went up in the mad zone.

Up and up and round and round it went. Through the villages, kids running out the way and chickens and goats. Missed the potholes. Up and up you went till you reckoned next stop was the sky. Carried on an hour like that, mountains on all sides only no-one took notice, like they clocked them every day. And they did, course. Then just when my stomach finally went cheerio we got there. World stopped spinning. Minibus stopped on the street by a square. We were in Mavis Bank. And still we were never near the top, still in the valley and mountains all round. Plenty of space upstairs.

I took a little recce. Mavis Bank looked like one big coffee factory and a couple of schools and a copshop and people walking up and down the road and yacking. Different from Kingston like sugar was different from shit. There were geezers going round cackling and giving it chat and not shooting each other.

And it was fucking beautiful you got to say.

I asked around for Miz Lucy. Least asked around the first person and she went straight off how I only got to go up the stalls round the corner and Miz Lucy she was there.

Went up the stalls, dozen or more selling bits and bobs.

Nothing to beat straight in. Women fanning themselves taking it quiet waiting for a busy time. Women clocking me under their porkies. Nothing to beat straight in.

'Scuse me ladies,' I goes, 'only I got to be looking for Miz Lucy.'

'Miz Lucy?'

'Miz Lucy?'

'Lady reckoned Miz Lucy was here. I got sent for Miz Lucy on account of her grandson name of Slip.'

Large pause.

Then a big old lady went 'I is Miz Lucy my friend. Do I hear you say you coming from my grandson?'

'As I'm stood here lady.'

'My my.' Then she went 'MY MY!' Then she went grinning wide 'You come over here from Slip?'

'Yes lady.'

Took her a while to think on all that. Then she went 'You come up here all alone like

153

that? You don't have no hire car?'

'No Miz Lucy.'

'So how you find me then?'

'Just asked Miz Lucy. Hope that all right with you.'

'Well!'

We had another little pause. Then she went 'So what your name my friend?'

'Nicky Miz Lucy.'

'Well let me tell you Mr Nicky don't you ask the way of any *man* in Jamaica you see? If you have to ask the way you ask a lady you hear? It dangerous you hear?'

'Dangerous?' I went.

'It dangerous!'

'Yeah dangerous plenty dangerous!' went her neighbour. 'You not hear about they tourists, they ask the way then men kill them and rob them and throw them away!'

'Do that in Walthamstow Miz Lucy,' I went.

'They friend you up then they take you in the bush then they kill you and rob you and throw you away!'

'Yeah Miz Lucy,' went that neighbour, 'and me tell you you cyaan tell by they looks. Some time they dress decent wear a necktie!'

'Eh Miz Patsy!'

'Hey,' went some lady seller over the road, 'Miz Lucy what you doing with that white man hey you put him down you hear!' Then she went something I never understood a word of and they all shook they cackled so much.

'Miz Angela!' went Miz Lucy. 'He talking. Miz Angela I telling you I love to *reason* with a white man. Me tell you I love to *reason* with a white man!' She gave me some big cake. 'Nicky friend you have a sugar bun or a coca bread, no?'

'Thank you Miz Lucy I wouldn't fight you off don't mind if I do.'

So I ate the big cake then she sent me off up the road on a little guesthouse not marked. Told me come back in the afternoon and she take me round hers and give me that meal and I tell her all the knockings on her grandson that Slip.

★　★　★

Guesthouse was another place they forgot the hot water when they put the plumbing in. Apart from that it was hunky. Never understood a fucking word the lady said only we came to arrangements on the notes we both understood. Then she gave me a cup of coffee, understood that too. Then I went out the edge of town for a walk round.

Plenty people walking. Or not walking.

'Morning,' I goes.

'Yes man yes.'

Bit further on.

'Hiya.'

'Yes man yes.'

Bit further on.

'Yes man yes.'

Two little girls about eight years old run up to me then stand there dumb. Little blue uniforms on the way home from school.

'My name's Nicky,' I goes. 'What about you?'

'Me called Alecia.'

'I is Valerie.'

Conversation stopped there a bit and we walked along with them three steps behind. We went on like that half a mile. Seemed they never got many geezers like me round there, bit like clocking an elephant.

'What you have for breakfast?' I goes trying to start things off again.

Made them giggle like it had to be a very silly question. Thought about trying to give the geezer an answer.

'Food!' went Alecia eventual.

Another conversation stopped.

Then Valerie went 'You got any daughters?'

'Reckon not.'

'You have a wife?'

'Bit young. Got a boy though Danny bit

156

younger than you.'

'Him a white boy?'

'Yeah him a white boy.'

'Oh.'

'Why you no have a wife?'

'Bit young. I got an ex-bird though that do?'

'What kind bird you have?'

'Er . . . a girlfriend, sort of, eh?'

'Oh.'

We walked on a bit then they went 'bye bye' and turned off and went down the hill.

Bit later I went back up Miz Lucy's.

*  *  *

Miz Lucy lived in some little wooden house on account of she was poor, only she kept it like the bleeding Ritz. Then she had her garden where she kept the veg.

'This my humble abode,' she went. 'This where that grandson spent he early years that rascal. He still a rascal that boy?'

'He still a rascal Miz Lucy.'

'Hmph. You want me show you my garden?'

There was never any saying no. Like showing a geezer a motor you got to clock it even you never interested. First garden I ever got a tour of come to that.

'This callaloo this carrot this plantain this pears this — '

'Scuse me Miz Lucy you got to go more slow,' I went. 'One thing I got to tell that Slip what you got in your garden. All I caught was carrot. We got them an' all. You want to go slow on them others?'

It was plantains and bananas and hot peppers. It was mangoes and pears we reckon are avocadoes, and tomatoes and carrots and lettuces. It was yams and sweet potatoes and callaloo and string beans and breadfruit. I wrote it all down for Slip. And a cow and chickens and a few goats. She had to be a busy lady Miz Lucy. Told her so. Hmph, she reckoned. Devil mek work fe idle hands. Lost me on that one only I never wanted to argue.

Then most the garden went in that meal. Most the vodka went down our throats. Time we finished we were best muckers you could reckon we went to school together. Told her all the doings round Walthamstow, she reckoned no different round Mavis Bank, plenty chasing the dosh and Saturday nights and a bit of the other. Only difference was it got hotter round Mavis Bank and you could go swimming Sundays in some mountain pool. Never do that round Walthamstow.

Told her all the story on that Slip. Ate some more. Time I staggered up the guesthouse it felt like I ate four meals. And it felt I got pissed up. Slip reckoned I only had to go back Miz Lucy after two days for meals. Not wrong Slip mate I reckoned, not wrong. Only trouble was when I got in I forgot all about why I went up Jamaica, only the evening it was a rave.

Then things happened stopped me getting back Miz Lucy at all.

# 9

I came out the guesthouse after four coffees looking for business. Miz Lucy gave me the info where the coffee plantations were, where was the factory and where they kept the old dark roast. Coffee plantations were up the mountain, high high and cloudy. So I went out the door with the export merchant viz on, stepped up the road for bumming a ride in some four-wheeler up the Blue Mountain. Early morning it was.

Jesus H Christ.

I clocked two bastards and a bitch out of Walthamstow.

Nah.

Was it good news?

Nah.

Landrover stopped up a roadside bar getting a 7-Up and asking questions. Two geezers asking the questions. Woman sat in the motor. Geezers were chief superintendent out of Chingford and Mickey Cousins who I met before. Chief Superintendent Armitage. Bird was Annabel Higgs, senior probation officer down the courts.

Go up and give them howdy?

You never could expect clocking three more unlikely characters. Chief super, probation boss and fucking millionaire motor trader? Do me a favour. See one of them here, no problem, entitled to their holidays. See two bloody remarkable coincidence. See three and it was a plan.

The question was, were they here on account of me?

I slipped back down a lane and waited. They gobbed their drinks and drove on towards getting up the mountain. I went up the snack bar.

'All right love?' I went.

'Good morning sir. You is wanting a soda?'

'Don't mind if I do love. You clocked them other English up there?'

'They is your friends?'

'They ask for me?'

'Big man with the moustache, he ask if he friend come this way. He say little squinty feller, sound a bit like you man.' She giggled.

'Big man's not my friend.'

'Oh. Perhaps you better make yourself small then you know?'

'Reckon that's a good idea love. They turn round and say where they was going?'

'Me think they just driving around looking for you. They said you was here coming after some business.'

161

Shit.

Little squinty feller supposed to mean? I never had a squint. Nor been little neither.

Shit. I never made any secret of going after coffee. Business round here meant coffee business. Folk asked what I was doing I told them coffee business.

But there was never any point turning back. Come out Jamaica then turn back on account of you met your probation officer's boss, bleeding comical.

So I copped a ride on a pickup going up the hill. Least I was walking past a pickup where the driver was sleeping dead to the world in his cab, then sudden it seemed he came to life, woke up all bouncy and got an urgent errand right up that same mountain where I was headed. For a special favour he might be persuaded on carrying me up there in the bargain.

'How much feller?' I goes.

'How much you want?'

Didn't help matters. Didn't help the negotiations.

'Hundred,' he went.

'Just cost me ten in the bus.'

'Yeah but you get me personal ride in comfort. And you get me quality conversation. And I is sincere. Not one hundred per cent sincere but I is sincere. And no buses go up there man.'

'You got a point at the end there geezer.'

So I climbed in his motor only found out then it came off the ark. Every pothole something fell off. And he drove that motor like he hated it.

'Easy John,' I goes. 'We get the other end maybe you buy a new motor with my cab fare. Meanwhile you got to treat her gentle you know? Like you loves her?'

'Listen my friend this is a piece of machinery. You treat a human being nice but you cyaan treat this machinery nice. It a piece of shit and you treat it like a piece of shit. No fuckin' around.'

'Fair enough John no problem.'

So we went up in the mountains. It was more of the same scenery only it got better. There were forests thick like they were jungle. There were waterfalls and birds whining like they were gone in a flash, hummingbirds. They got orange trees and grapefruit trees and banana trees and coffee bushes. Plenty coffee bushes. They got coffee beans drying in the factory yard, coffee beans drying round back gardens, coffee beans drying by the road. Geezers carrying bleeding great loads on their Judge Dreads, old biddies too looked like they ought to be in rest homes not humping sacks of veg. There was a wind blew down the mountain and a wind blew up the mountain and the sun was shining. I got bumped up left my seat about a thousand times on the trip, still the same happened to the driver never seemed to bother him, drove in mid-air half the time. He reckoned he was delivering a few groceries round some lodge up there about four thousand feet up. I hoped he never crashed down the mountainside, be a shame they never got their groceries.

Miz Lucy told me I got to go far far up the mountain for that coffee. Seemed like a fair place to start then. Same time maybe I could clock the Walthamstow hostiles before they clocked me. They knew the story was coffee, only they never knew I was ahead of the game, got there first and already spotted them.

The driver turned off and stopped. I got down shaking and went thanks and doshed him his bucks. Now how did I find them small farmers?

Never needed to fret. Three of them found me under ten seconds.

'Yeah man,' went one.

'Nice, man.'

'Morning,' I went.

'Yeah man. You climbing up the mountain?'

'Do me a favour,' I went.

'Where you from?'

'Walthamstow,' I went.

'You want to buy coffee?'

'Morning,' I started again. 'You geezers got to be small farmers?'

'Small small farmers.'

'Then you geezers is just the geezers I come after.'

'Nice, man.'

'How'd you reckon if we went somewhere got a quiet cup of tea talked business eh?'

'Bush tea?'

'Er . . . you smoke that?'

'Drink tea man.'

'Maybe we get a coffee eh?'

We went in that lodge, like a couple of old houses. Few geezers milling around swishing their machetes looking busy. Few other geezers digging holes in the ground got muscles like in a prison gym. Me I walked up there with those small farmers giving the viz on a serious attitude. They reckoned I was a tourist. Even I never wore shorts. All my days I had trouble getting respect that was due a geezer with heavy views.

We sat down. By now me and seven or eight small farmers.

'Gents,' I turned round and said. 'My name's Nicky.'

'Nice, Nicky, nice,' young dude went.

'All right Nicky?'

'Yeah man Nicky.'

'Yeah well,' I went, 'I'm from England innit?'

'No!' They all fell about. 'We thought you was from Japan man!'

I had to cackle. After that we were all right, able to do the business.

Down in Kingston I popped in a supermarket near the buses, never believed my mince pies at the price on the coffee. Ganja was less. Up here coffee was half the price only from what I clocked on the road still big man prices. Never wanted to get turned over on the deal so I went to work on the charm school.

'Fellers,' I went, 'I got a mate back in England reckons you small farmers getting ripped off by the Board.'

'Ripped off,' went a geezer they called Basil, grey straggly beard woolly hat cracked all the jokes, serious geezer.

'Ripped off,' they all went.

'Now I got to give you the SP,' I turned round and said. I sipped the coffee they gave me from the pot, made my hair curl. 'I ain't got a fuckin' clue what I'm doing here and you fellers could go rumping me round the cleaners no danger. Only I reckon maybe we can get some kind of arrangement here, I scratch you and you scratch me type of thing.

I'm after this coffee game, export, top style Blue Mountain, just a taste for starters see how it goes eh? We reckon me and my mate Slip we start little little then build up, give us a slice give you a slice and miss out on the Board, you hear what I'm saying?'

'Hey man,' went Basil.

'Yeah?'

'Where the fire, man?'

'Pardon?'

'Slow down, chile, slow down, drink you coffee, you walk too fast. Give me a headache.'

'Oh, right.' We sat there drank our coffee till his headache went off. They stretched their feet maybe thought about their vegetables growing.

Then Basil went 'Now Nicky, you say Slip. You say Slip?'

'Yeah Slip.'

'Him related to Miz Lucy's grandson out of Mavis Bank went England?'

'Yeah that Slip! You know the geezer?'

He slapped his leg and laughed. 'Me know him? Me know him? Me knew him when he was pickney. Him still a rascal?'

'Still a rascal,' I went, and we all cackled. Then they all yacked between themselves and cackled some more only I never understood a word of it.

'Him visit Miz Lucy maybe two year ago, wanted to set up export business?'

'That the picture,' I went. 'Only like he's out of circulation a while so he sent me sort of a partner.'

'And you all know good what he planned that Slip?' Basil went to them. 'We tell him buy the coffee man, sell it up England. And you hear what he got in his mind? Buy the ganja and export it in them little coconuts!' He slapped his leg again and fell about. They all slapped their legs and fell about. Give it half an hour and plenty falling about and maybe we might start doing business again.

'So he sent me instead like,' I goes to remind them, 'being as how I'm his mate and his export licence ain't cool just now. Only this time he reckoned he fancied that coffee of yours, you catch my drift?'

Nodding and shaking heads, yacking among themselves.

'Catch the feller's drift,' went someone.

'So where he be out of circulation?' went Basil sudden.

'Well . . . '

'Prison?'

'Since you mention it like.'

'For that ganja?'

'Like.'

'Hah!' More cackling all round. Me I

couldn't wait for telling Slip the fun he gave the neighbours. Still it looked like we might be in. Never mind the cackling they were in the game.

'Nicky my friend,' went Basil. 'Me think we might be able to come to some arrangement here. You sit here have some more coffee and we make up some plans you hear?'

More of that coffee and I was likely going into orbit. But we sat there and made the plans.

Explained for a start it was like an experiment, test the water, take what I could carry, suss out the delicatessens and coffee shops back home. Top quality gear only see what we could flog. Maybe this time since it was only a bit off the back, miss out on troubling the export licence geezers. We got a market then we could do the business, even paper business know what I mean.

We got a deal. We shook the hands. They reckoned on talking up other small farmers, geezers got maybe a couple of acres. First they'd bring me some beans down Mavis Bank for collecting. Big man name of Oscar was due there next day so he'd meet me outside the post office midday. Me I'd take all I could carry, top quality gear only. We settled on the price no problem.

I was so happy I near as shit myself. Not

only I could make Slip very happy, it was legit work. Well, legit after a fashion. Legit maybe next time when we paid import and taxes and shit. For now it was legit-ish. Might even get me cred with that Noreen.

Then I walked back out on the path and as near as had another fucking heart attack.

They were there and this time they clocked me.

# 10

They were on foot about a hundred yards off, must have left the landrover round the corner.

'Hey!' yelled Armitage. 'You, Burkett!'

I never wanted to know. Only I knew now for definite. They were here on account of me.

Try and work it all out later. Meanwhile get the fuck out.

They were downhill of me and so was their motor, back the way I came up. Only other way was up the path going uphill. Going in after the small farmers for help never look so dandy, oops scuse me fellers I know we just made a deal here only there's a few geezers seem to be after my locks. Only way then was upstairs up that mountain.

And fuck me there was a bit of luck here. A guided party going up that mountain, four white geezers and two white birds and a black guide. Just my opportunity for pulling a stroke here.

I ran up behind them.

'Scuse me fellers, ladies,' I goes.

'Hey how you doin'? How are you?' Yanks.

171

'Goin' up this mountain fellers, ladies, only I wonder you could do me a small favour let me join you up there a bit eh?'

'Sure, sure, you just tag along with us. You just tag along right here. You going up the peak?'

Fuck me, Yanks, I almost preferred Scousers, still you can't always be choosers. I got right in the middle of their babble and smiled at them like a toyboy and never even looked back. Fuckers back there wanted me. Wanted me to turn round and talk about something I never wanted to turn round and talk about, whatever it was.

So I nestled in those Yanks. Then would you believe it turned up they were fucking missionaries there in Jamaica. Missionaries? Every second Jamaican a vicar and they still got missionaries? Anyway, entitled to their problems I reckoned. We got walking up that mountain and I was panting. Panting from fear and very soon panting from that bleeding mountain.

* * *

You ever climbed up a mountain? Pain was never in it. Sweat fell off me in little puddles. We climbed up there and we climbed up there some more and I was far gone totalled

172

and they reckoned we were nowhere near half way. I got dirt on my Reeboks. I got sniped by a mosquito. I could feel my hooter getting hotter and redder in that sun till it was nowhere near a fashion item. Then the path went in the jungle and out the sun, only that was no better when some creeper made a lunge at me and scratched me all down my good looks. I reckoned next was going to be some hummingbird thought I was a flower and pecked my little mince pies out. All the while my T-shirt got wetter and wetter under the sweat and the panting got shorter and shorter. And shorter still. Jesus there was geezers did this for fun. Reckon you got to have exercise I favoured a good all-nighter some rave up the club, dance all night, take a few Es and don't forget several pints of water and you never even got cream crackered in the bargain.

After about three years we got halfway up where there was a ranger station. My party went off for a bit of a drink-up in the snacker before they carried on.

I never knew what was my best plan next, hide up there or carry on with the God squad up the mountain. First off though I knew I was never clocking the Superpig and friends behind me so I went round the corner for a bit of a forty winks in the shade. Knackered I was. So I sat down there like Mr Cool knew exactly what was going down in the world, and then would you believe it, like a total plonker I fell sound asleep. I was out of it. I was away.

And I dreamed about seven pints of lager and a packet of cheese and onion.

It was lovely.

Then I woke up with a fucking great jerk when some fucking mosquito started a bleeding blood transfusion on my ear.

I got up like a shotgun and went back up by the path. No-one around, not a ranger not a fucking missionary, never get one when you wanted. No-one.

Jesus this was stupid. Not a place to be leaving yourself on your tod. I set off back to that path fast to catch up with the missionaries again, lovely sweet missionaries listen to their jabber all day when they want. Then when I moved away from the trees and across the open ground I heard noises coming from around the ranger hut. Not God-type noises more like pig-type noises. I moved faster they moved faster. Turned round and there they were. Chief super, motor trader, probation boss. They were there for me.

And they never came to tell me my library books were overdue.

'You! Burkett! Stop right there!' Armitage again. 'You and us, we need to talk.'

'Up yours copper, you got to be joking.'

'Take that attitude and we shall get nowhere. Do some talking and we can sort this out.' They were coming closer across the space, I was backed against a tree, reached the path now. 'You're stepping on toes here Burkett you're on dangerous ground. What do you think you're trying to do here eh? Muscle in on other people's water?' He came closer still. 'Better start the conversation don't you think? Talk and we might be able to sort something out here. What do you say then eh?'

'Fuck yourself is what I say. Think I'd talk to you? Came here for a talking did you? Get a fucking grip here pig do yourself a favour.' I was away.

And they came.

And they made themselves busy somewhere on the gardening tools. They borrowed someone's machetes. Everyone round that country carried a machete, only they used it on their banana trees not waving it about like doing some very serious damage. It was shitting time for me, heavy shitting time. They meant to waste me.

I ran up that path going up the mountain. I ran. When it got in the trees it was wet and slippery. I was quicker than them only I fell, got up, slipped again. I got up and ran like the clappers up the path into the forest only I knew I was in trouble there. Hear their footsteps and their panting then I slipped again and fuck me they were there.

I got up and away from them, then a sudden tearing, crying pain tore my shoulder in half, oh fuck. I was down, rolled over and up again. They missed me next time, got a rock. There was only one way out though or else they got me for sure. Up the path and I was finished. Over the edge and I stood a chance, down the mountain and into the jungle away from them. It was never a choice. I jumped.

Another strike glanced off me when I jumped, lucky bastard I was. I was into the bush. I was falling, plunging, tearing, starting to try pushing stuff on one side. I stumbled into a tree, then bamboo, legs wading through creepers and bushes and the whole fucking jungle. I heard them just after, crashing and slashing, swearing and cutting. They got the machetes only I was desperate, dead meat if they got me. I never met anyone before wanted to total me. I never liked it. I was away.

I fell twenty, thirty times dropping down the hillside. Grab a branch and it had thorns on, tore my mitts up made me cry out. Creeper wrapped round my throat yanked me backwards. Another branch whacked me in the gob. Thistles like daggers stung my legs straight through my strides. Rashes spread on my skin everywhere instant, least of my worries. Ants bit when I fell on them, grass cut my ankles, I came to a full stop in thick bamboo. Came out again, went round, stumbled further on down. It seemed like it went on forever.

Then I stopped. No sound they were following. I sat and gasped, shaking, fucking terrified.

Then I inspected the damage.

Jesus.

Through the T-shirt the shoulder flapped open, bleeding regular. I tied the shirt over for holding it in and keeping the dirt out. Next I clocked the wound on the other arm, sliced nicely only not so deep, no major problem. I got to get down though soon.

So I started off again more gentle and then I hit on a stream. Jesus they must have said some prayer for me the missionaries. All streams supposed to go downhill so I heard and they reckoned you could never get lost then. Only they forgot the signposts on this one. I was lost.

In the bargain I was well and truly fucked.

They forgot the stepping stones same time they forgot the signposts, so when I followed the water down I was falling with it, slipping and sliding and cursing with it. I fell and cracked my nut on a stone. I got blisters in my shoes from the water. Twenty minutes or more it went on like that, slipping and sliding and cursing and aching and weeping. Then would you believe all of a sudden I was in banana fields.

And coffee bushes and oranges would you credit it. Jesus. They must have made a fucking burnt offering for me when they did that prayer. I went ballistic. Least I went what passed for ballistic round then for me, I made a little smile and went 'fuck me gently'. I reckoned I was going to be alive.

★ ★ ★

From the fields there had to be tracks where they took the veg home. I found one and kept going. It went past a hut, just a hut for your tea break and keeping your bananas in. I kept on down the track and it got more like a road. Found another hut. Only this time it was never a hut more like a house. There were sounds.

I went up and knocked on the door.

Geezer came round from the back where

he was digging something. He clocked my shoulder straight off, went 'Hey man you're hurt'. Then he got the viz on the rest of it, everything torn and filthy and blood on it, and he went 'Hey man you need help, come in here come in'.

Then before I did his missis came out and went 'oh', bit of a surprise like. Then the next thing I knew, before we even got a cup of tea and talked about the weather everything went all wavy and I was sliding slowly slowly down on the floor. Shit, I reckoned, only there was never a fucking thing I could do.

Then sudden, just before I went out sleeping proper, I got a mighty, bleary fix on it all.

In one part of my brain I heard that Armitage going 'You! Burkett! Stop right there!'

Then the other part of my brain I heard The Voice when it belled me up my gaff. It went 'Burkett?' Then it went 'Burkett I've got news for you'. Then it went 'Maybe you ought to look up your girlfriend'.

Chief Fucking Superintendent Armitage was The Voice.

★ ★ ★

When I finished my little snooze they already got me a drink of water and a blanket and the missis was washing the big cut. Cloud of little insects was coming out of it. 'Christ Almighty,' I turned round and said a bit weak, 'Jesus lady that hurts only thanks'.

'You is wanting a doctor quick,' went the geezer. 'I sent my boy for a pickup.'

'Thanks man. Thanks a bunch both of you. Oo er.' I felt woozy.

Another geezer arrived straight away in a pickup, small boy with him. 'Huh,' he went clocking the state of me. 'Take you the doctor.'

I thought about it. 'I know a doctor,' I went. Took a drink of that water they held for me. Shaking all over couldn't halt it. 'You reckon you can go to Widcombe?'

'Widcombe!' he went like it was China. 'It is far off. Maybe ten miles.'

'Be brave, eh?' I goes. 'Thirty US be fair?'

'Talking!' he goes. 'I do it for nothing you understand because you hurt man, but do it quicker for thirty US!'

'We go for it then eh?'

I got the geezer and his missis with the hut to write their names and address. Then I got the doc's card out my pocket where I kept it. Got it out with the arm not missing a flap. Showed it the driver, name of Tony.

'He have a number there too,' he went. 'You want I ring him on the earphone?'

'Carphone!'

'Sure man I have a earphone. Use it at work. I just having my lunch break now when they fetch me. This doctor probably having his lunch break now too. You want I try him at his number?'

'Yeah.'

He dialled the number and a woman's voice came on. He passed the receiver to the good arm.

'Jane?' I went.

'No, this is her mother, who is this?'

'Oh I'm sorry lady, any chance the doc's home, only my name's Nicky and I need a doctor urgent.'

'Hold on a minute please. He is sleeping. Hold on one moment.'

The doc came on in a bit. 'Who is that? Is that my young friend Nicky?'

'Doc I'm on the road in a pickup. I been hurt. Sorry real sorry only I need you kind of urgent, kind of bad.'

'Come straight here. Let me speak to whoever is driving, please.'

So Tony took directions, went 'yeah man' about twenty times. Then I fell asleep still holding my shoulder together, and when I woke up again we were in the driveway of a California palace.

'Now here is another one, Nicky,' went the

doc when he stuck the eighty-first needle in me.

'Jesus Doc this bush medicine or what sticking pins in geezers?'

'I see you have not lost your sense of humour young man but perhaps you should not try me too far when I am sticking those pins in you.'

'Right Doc.'

'Now I have given you inoculations and antibiotics and local anaesthesia and so next I shall set about the sutures that you need.' We already agreed on him doing it, least he agreed on him doing it not the hospital. Fortunate he kept his surgery next door and reckoned he could manage. I never wanted every cop round Jamaica getting involved.

Fucking great flap on the shoulder no danger only he reckoned he could fix it up. 'It is very fortunate,' he went, 'very fortunate indeed, considering the force of the blow, that it was struck at an angle. If it had been someone who was used to wielding a machete, say a banana farmer, I suspect that your arm would not still be with us. Even so you may need hospital treatment later if the skin does not bind.'

'Telling me I ought to be thankful Doc.'

'Well, something like that. The other arm will be less problematic because it was truly only a glancing blow. A half dozen stitches in that one, perhaps. Then we shall have to dress your scratches and grazes and bites. In addition I believe you are suffering from shock. I think you should stay here tonight, but meanwhile when I have finished treating you I think I should call the police.'

'Oh no Doc.' Thought we avoided that.

'Oh no what?'

'Oh no Doc not them police. I never get on with them police Doc. Not nowhere.'

'Hmmm.'

'And I want them people back home Doc. Do my own bit of policing like.'

'You mean gain the help of the local constabulary? They could not arrest someone for deeds in another country unless that country's police force had been involved first you know.'

'I was thinking more of like unofficial constabulary Doc. Know quite a few unofficial constabulary like to land their mitts on that Mickey Cousins was up there. Never want them to know we were making official actions first, could get them leery know what I mean?'

'Hmmm.'

'And they cover up their actions Doc after they get lifted, then we never find out the doings eh?'

'Nicky I will give it some thought and decide where my duty lies. First, though, I believe you need some rest.'

So then he stitched me head to foot near as, put the dressings on head to foot, got some of that herb tea supposed to cure everything headaches to leprosy, then he went off after the afternoon's grafting. His missis helped me up their spare room then I clocked that bed and I fell asleep before I lay down. I was out of it.

★ ★ ★

When I woke up that Jane was there, her little mince pies right in front of mine.

'Roll me up if it ain't Jane or I'm dreaming,' I went all sleepy. 'Christ I hurt all over. Christ you aren't half a smart looking totty Jane.'

'Oh Nicky,' she went, 'you poor boy.' Now that was what a geezer needed, no-one told me that in about twenty years.

'Say that again,' I goes.

'No I won't, I don't want to spoil you. But you sleep now and you can tell me all about it when you wake up again.'

So I slept. I dreamed I fell down a mountain of blood. I dreamed I got slashed by a hummingbird with a razor beak then chased over a lake of coffee by my probation officer with a warrant and a harpoon. I dreamed they were gobbling my shoulders with yam and plantains and hot sauce. Then I woke up again. It was dark.

This time the doc was there. 'You all right Nicky?' he went. 'You want some more bush tea maybe?'

'No Doc no!' I went, reckoned the bush tea caused the nightmares. 'Fine I'm fine Doc honest, only leave me be and I'm fine Doc, thanks Doc eh?'

Then I slept till morning. No nightmares, nothing, only six o'clock breaking and cocks crowing and dogs barking like always. Six o'clock meant I slept fifteen hours all told. And Jane never reckoned I was a poor boy again.

# 11

Doc Francis came in and pulled back the curtains. 'Good morning Nicky,' he went, 'it is eight o'clock and it is Saturday. How are you feeling?'

It was cool in there with that air conditioning. Except my body hurt from the top of my bonce down the tip of my plates I felt like a million bucks. I was in Hollywood. They were bringing me freshly squeezed orange juice like in the adverts.

'Doc,' I went. 'I got a feeling you might be God.'

'No I'm not, although he is a close relative you know. Do you think you can get up?'

'Give it a go.' I tried getting out of the bed, cried out loud then fell back again.

'Gimme five Doc,' I went. 'Be with you soon I reckon.' I tried again, never cried out quite so loud. I slipped the legs out, saw someone some time took all my clothes off, oh well. Then clocked there were bits of blood all over me, Christ all over their sheets. 'Oh shit,' I went. And bits of mud and bush everywhere in the bargain and probably a few hummingbirds and lizards and snakes in there, no, Jamaica never got snakes.

'Think you can make it to the bath?'

'No problem. No worries. Yah! Hope I never block the drain is all.'

'The bathroom is just through this door. Here is a towel. I have placed a disposable razor there if you think you are able to shave. Do not get the cuts on your shoulders wet, do you hear? The little cuts and scratches do not matter. You can put antiseptic on them when you get out of the bath.'

Even my mum never gave me a razor. Sent me down the bleedin' shop.

'Be just fine Doc, feeling just dandy now.' Then I cried out again.

'Join us downstairs for a late breakfast when you can.' Late meant eight o'clock when only tourists still laid in bed. So he went off.

No need going into detail on that bath. Once I got in it looked out of the question I ever got out again. Only I did. Fucking like a hero. Then I wiped antiseptic cream all over me so I was shiny. Like lubricated ready for anything.

Tried shaving only gave it up after one side. Cleaned the teeth including getting the ants out. Combed the hair like shaking a tree.

Then I went downstairs in the clothes he left out for me. Only a holiday shirt and

187

shorts like a fucking Yankee.

'Hi,' I went.

They all fell about. Only Jane fell about noisily, other two kept their smirking a bit quieter. I felt like a Bosnian refugee they kitted out off the Oxfam shop.

'Do sit down please,' went Mrs Doc. 'I do believe we have not been properly introduced. My name is Catherine. Please make yourself completely at home you know.'

'I reckon I got to be in a video,' I went sitting down. 'Orange juice and air conditioning and folks introduce themselves. Pardon me I don't shake hands missis only I reckon I might need a painkiller after.' Then I did sit down slowly feeling pretty stupid, then it all got a bit better when that Jane started giggling again and going 'look at the state of you' and then they all set off cackling and slapping their table and then I started too only that hurt in the bargain.

I drank the orange juice. Couldn't eat only half a cold pancake lying there, just the biz.

'After breakfast I will make sure of your wounds again,' went the doc. 'First you eat what you can, though, then I think it might be helpful if you told us what you know of the causes of your predicament here in Jamaica.'

So I gave it to them. Everything I knew.

Even about being in a prison cell with that Slip.

* * *

Far as I could tell it was like this.

I got released. Then George the warrant offered me. He offered me on account of Rameez was whacked, and on account of a cop got shafted. Some reason they reckoned it was connected with me. They reckoned I'd get back for Rameez. They reckoned while I was busy on that I'd turn up the geezer whacked the filth. In the picture they also had a little chancer on me and the boys getting it sorted.

Unofficial. Over the counter the Bill were doing it by the book. On the side they wanted it sorted, and no objection paying for it.

Till now I reckoned it was all connected with me too, only not the way they measured it.

Did my bird and all I wanted when I got out was the big snooze. Down the boozer, put it up a few birds, maybe take a glance on Slip's Jamaican deal. Safe. Rameez got done stepping on someone's toes, his problem. Take him his flowers only he never asked me getting involved. DS fucking Grant got smacked, no worries. More business Interflora.

189

Then it all started looking different, nothing I put in a request for only it was my name in the frame. First I got noticed in a post office. Then Jimmy Foley got burned on the videos and our Sharon got warned. Then Dean and George and me all got knocked and finished up next to Rameez, drinking out the same teapot. Then Noreen got sliced. Then I got followed up Jamaica. I reckoned it was a conspiracy, everyone reckoned it was a conspiracy and I was the plot. Only I lost the plot.

'I reckon it's a conspiracy,' I turned round and said. Only while I was saying it I was thinking. For what they followed me up Jamaica? First they warned me, tried warning me off. Then maybe it got in heavy water like with DS fucking Grant, they got spotted they got identified, so they tried for the big carvery.

'I reckon it's a conspiracy only I never done the right thinking before,' I went. 'Never put it together like till now sat here sipping with the old orange juice.'

'How do you mean Nicky?'

'Till now I only reckoned someone put a hit on me, some reason I never knew. Only now you clock it from the outside, it weren't only me. True I knew the geezers got hit, only I know plenty other geezers aren't hit. How about for starters we were all doing a little piece of work on their patch?'

'Whose patch?'

'Fuck knows . . . Oh, bugger me Mrs Doc, shit . . . I mean I got to apologise it just slipped out . . . '

'That's quite all right Nicky, you were concentrating. Do carry on please.'

'Dunno whose patch. Dunno until now any road. Chief Superintendent and Senior Probation and Mickey Cousins. You reckon there's more? You reckon it ain't me they're after, only anyone steps on their piece of work? You reckon they got a closed market don't want anyone stepping in it? You got a thinking maybe they control everything, they warning the rest on not getting involved?'

'Tell us more, Nicky.'

I got to swallow thinking on it. Swallowing hurt the same as breathing. Still swallowed.

'There was a post office. Post offices are very large dosh. Often connected to Class A drugs. Anyone got a sawnoff holds up a post office, only they run in rashes. Someone sticks a whole lot then it dies down, everyone cool. Nice racket. Maybe there's got to be someone in control, makes the mark where it happens and when. Not impressed with any geezer starts interfering the plans.'

I swallowed some more and did the thinking.

'Then motors is very big dosh indeed. Maybe they never minded when little geezers was lifting Astras and Golfs for that Rameez. Only then he got ambitious, started out on them Jeeps and Porsches. Then he got a problem, and a problem put him in the hospital. They wanted them Jeeps and Porsches no interruptions. Bang 'em up straight off in them containers down Tilbury, in the case and abroad before they hunt down that tracker they put in these days, beep beep. They making very big bananas on them Porsches and whatsits. Then Rameez step in, he not only lifts a Jag, then they take it over and he got to come after them. So they start out feeling threatened, you catch my drift?

'Then too much of a coincidence, Dean got cut and Jimmy got shot up when both of them got nice little numbers working for them. Maybe they were stepping on someone's toes, some nice big merchandising they already got set up and performing.

'My guess I got to ask our Sharon a few questions when I get back, what she setting up round the estates. My guess it ain't only her being my sister got her warned.

'Then the final deal is they get the message on me going up Jamaica. They reckon I got to be stepping in. Loungers, they got a deal on loungers? Deckchairs ruin their market? Nah. They reckon I got to be after ganja or crack, bit of import. So they come after me, see the knockings, maybe rub me out. Jesus. It got to be it.'

I did a lot of thinking. Some of it came to me in the night. Some of it came in the bath. Some of it came when I just laid it all out for them like for the first time. Now I was even more tired.

'Stupid really,' I went. 'All we're after is a bit of work like. Me I'm wanting a quiet life now. Last thing we want is muscling in on them. Never even knew they were there, like organised all round. Then what do we find only they want us out their manor, and out their manor in a box. Ain't cool, ain't cool at all. They got an arrangement you ask me. Got it all sowed up, business in Walthamstow, all divvied between them and they never let no-one take a share. Try for the big time and you get warned. Get in the way serious and you get whacked very heavy.'

The doc and his missis and that Jane all sipped their orange juice. What you did on Saturday morning, you sipped your orange juice. Then the doc spoke.

'It seems to me,' he went, 'as if they may be getting desperate, as if they really think you are a threat to them. Anyone who would use a machete, anyone white who would want to use a machete in Jamaica, is getting desperate. It is true that out in the country here we still get attacks with machetes, but the typical murder these days is done by force of the gun. But as foreigners they had no guns. I regret to say that I believe they intended to murder you young Nicky. If they had tipped you into the bush after killing you on the path you could remain undiscovered for weeks, even months.'

'Bleedin' having a laugh eh. Here you go, book your hols in Jamaica, expect a bit of robbing and that, all you get's folk out of Walthamstow come over reckon you're stepping on some toes so you got to get carved up.'

So we sipped some more of that orange juice and I got it followed by about eighteen cups of that coffee. Me I still never knew the difference from Nescaff except it was ten times stronger, only everyone round there reckoned it got to be the best in the world no danger. Not for me to argue.

Speaking of which I had a load of coffee being delivered midday in Mavis Bank.

The doc reckoned he'd go after it. Had to be one brilliant geezer that doc, think he'd got nothing else for making himself busy

Saturday. Meet the feller Oscar outside the post office midday. Give him the SP on the situation. Oscar bound to believe him on account of he was legit. Doc gives him the dosh, exchange for the coffee. Then get my bag out the guesthouse and pay the lady two nights. Everyone happy. Probably the Walthamstow fuckers were out of there, only in any case I was scarce.

And no talk of Old Bill.

'Sweet, Doc,' I went. 'Owe you one mate.'

'You're welcome. Now I gone.'

And he was too.

★ ★ ★

The doc was gone a couple of hours. When he came back he was cackling.

'Oh boy I hope you like coffee young Nicky,' he goes, 'and I hope everyone you know likes coffee. You realise how much you bought here?'

'I just ordered some coffee Doc like a bagful.'

'I think you have a bagful. I hope the bag will go on the aeroplane.'

He unloaded it off the back of the motor. Motor smelled of coffee. Street smelled of coffee. He got it in the front room. House smelled of coffee.

Slip told me take an empty bag. Just one change of clothes was it. Now we stuffed that big bag full of coffee beans till it was busting, then we filled two carrier bags out of Food Giant I brought from home on account of I heard they never got carriers abroad. They were big carriers like it was a big travel bag. Then when they were full I gave the rest of the beans to the doc and Mrs Doc.

First they refused, reckoned it was too much only then I threatened on marrying their daughter if they never accepted, so they changed their mind right quick. Fact they ground some of the beans there and then so we got a cuppa. Another cuppa.

Still tasted just like coffee to me nothing ultra. They reckoned it was such hot shit though I never turned round and said different.

One thing though that coffee never kept me awake. Gave me the shakes only still never kept me awake. Did my shakings sleeping. Maybe I slept on account of one arm was throbbing and my brain was throbbing and the whole body moaning and both arms were in slings. I never did a lot of pressups. Then again maybe it was the little sleepers the doc gave me. Any event I was out of it, went to my pit for two days and only came out for mealtimes.

I offered to go up some guesthouse. Still a few days till that big bird went home so I offered. Never meant it for real so a bit fortunate they never listened. Sucked their teeth and frowned at me as it goes.

'Nicky,' went Mrs Doc, 'you are our guest. We would not think of you going anywhere else, especially in the condition you are in now, you hear?'

Then that Jane giggled. 'Anyway Nicky,' she went, 'let you out in Kingston you probably start a gang war inside two days. You're not safe man, you're a danger to the community.'

'Jane,' went the doc, 'I do believe you are making fun of young Nicky again, and he is still a sick man you know.'

'Yeah but look at the state of him,' she goes, 'you've got to make fun of him isn't that right?'

'He should stay here,' goes the doc, 'and he should stay peaceful and untroubled for a day or two while his body and his mind recover.'

Me I stayed cool.

When I got out of bed without a hydraulic I sat at the patio and gawped at the mountains and got the bandages sunburned. Then when I reckoned I could walk round a bus it seemed like it was time to go view the sights, check the country like and get out of their hair a couple of days.

So the doc gave permission when I seemed like half way human, far as I'd ever be.

So I went.

\* \* \*

I went round Jamaica. Jane took me down the bus station reckoned she wanted to see me safe out or she'd never credit it. Got me my ticket for Montego Bay. I wanted to glide in Montego Bay like Mr Invisible. I heard about Mo Bay, I heard you stopped to tie a shoelace and there was thirty geezers wanted to be your friend take you on a tour.

Got there and found it was more like a hundred and thirty. All very friendly wanted to be your best mucker.

First that bus went up Ocho Rios, big hotels and a ship in. Sun shone. Then Ocho Rios up Montego Bay, big hotels and a ship in. Sun shone. I shook off the geezers, told them I never wanted no friends thank you. Bought a T-shirt. Went through the tourist strip, clocked a few tourists. Then up by the airport and stopped in a guesthouse the doc already booked me in. They still forgot the hot water.

Then I went down by the beaches. Wore my new T-shirt, spot of Marcus Garvey.

Never took it off though nor my jeans, case the locals took a mind to cackle over my body. I did a bit of scouting round for deckchairs, business-style.

Beach was no problem as it goes, everyone was cool. Rest of the borough was nothing but agg, one big no-no. I got a pizza up Shakey's and went back by the guesthouse, spent the evening watching basketball on the TV with the night man.

Next day was more of that coffee for breakfast, then the bus out of Montego Bay for Negril. Little hotels and no ship in, nowhere to put it. Sun still shone. Negril was the spot, no problem no pain. I got four pieces of cake and a box drink then another bus up Kingston. That was Jamaica.

★   ★   ★

I belled Jane from Negril, told her the time we got in if we got lucky. Then spent the trip yacking about cricket, rather listening about cricket on account of I know fuck all about cricket. Geezer I sat next to told me about matches he saw not only before I was born but before he was born. Probably still yacking now. Then when we got in Jane was waiting for me in the motor, save me getting shafted round the bus station this time.

'Yo Jane,' I went, waving bye to the talker.

'Hello Nicky,' she went, giving me a little kiss on the cheek made my teeth chatter. Only problem was she never wanted to kiss me anywhere else that Jane. 'How you doing then?' she went smiling, laughing and friendly made me just too glad to see her. 'You seen our beautiful country then?'

'Slip was right and he was wrong,' I turned round and said.

'He was?'

'He was. There ain't no deckchairs on the public beaches. Hire them out make a killing, deckchair attendant millionaire. Only one trouble is, round the private hotels they got deckchairs coming out their arses. I ain't never clocked nothing like it. They got to be antiques they exported along of the motors when they ain't got no more useful life. Tell you it ain't only loungers like we thought, they got them too, only they got them real deckchairs . . .'

'Jesus Nicky,' she turned round and said. 'Deckchairs! You still going on about deckchairs!'

'True words. Deckchairs in all them hotels. Public beaches though them punters just lie down get sand up their fannies. Primitive you ask me.'

'Christ.'

'I done Jamaica now.'

'Oh, you noticed Jamaica apart from the deckchairs then?'

'Been there. Rice and peas, rum punch, pizza, tasty Jamaica birds eye you up. Anything else I got to do before I get on that plane?'

Then she registered I was winding her up so she leaned over and whacked me. Prefer she kissed me again only she whacked me. Whacked me on the only place not still bruised, my gob. 'So how have you been Nicky?' she went. 'Do you hurt still, man?'

'Yeah. Most all over Jane, only gets better. Your dad not only got to be a diamond he seems like he's one sharp quack in the bargain, eh?'

'I think he's a very good doctor, yes. I'm glad. So tell me, what did you think of the island and its scenery then?'

'Scenery's fucking brilliant Jane. Got to be ace. That Mo Bay though, Christ what a pit.'

'Well as a matter of fact I might agree with you there.'

Then we got home. That night slept in my bed again and we got that orange juice and coffee and the rest again. We just had one more talking me and Jane. On account of she was a woman she wasn't about to let it rest there.

* * *

We had our tea that night me and the doc
and his missis and Jane, then she took me out
to a hotel for a drink, celebrate me leaving
them. We drove downtown or uptown, one or
the other. Then that hotel had palm trees
outside and carpets inside like a mattress. Air
conditioning like an icebox after the street.
Atmosphere much the same.

Geezers in uniform crept up very quiet on
you, make you nervous. Spoke very quiet,
mixed your drinks very quiet and took your
dosh very quiet. No hotels like that round
Walthamstow.

'They swallow their drink in here Jane?' I
went. 'Or they just inhale it?'

She cackled. 'They do say the people who
come in here, their shit don't smell,' she
went. 'Now you can buy me a nice long drink
Nicky please. Maybe a daiquiri since we are
in this kind of place.' Even Jane she spoke
posher in there, kind of hushed.

I wandered off looking for the bar. Geezer
reckoned I wanted the toilet, pointed the way
and I started out for it only Jane called me
back. 'Nicky,' she went, 'they come round and
take your order here, it's not like a pub.'

'Right on Jane no problem. Sit tight then.'
So they came over and did the quiet bit

stooping, and Jane ordered her daiquiri and I got a rum with everything, kind of a fruit and veg flan without the pastry. Amount of ice on top added to their aircon brought serious danger of frostbite.

'Now we can have a talk,' went Jane.

My experience birds wanted to have a talk meant very heavy duty. Preferred CID less aggravation. Jane got her serious viz on.

'Deckchairs?' I went. 'You changed your mind on them deckchairs Jane, reckon we got a market and you want in on the deal?'

She sucked her molars. Made a noise somewhere between a rattlesnake and my mum when you threw up over the washing. Kind of venomous.

'I guess you were on about some other subject,' I went.

'Nicky,' she turned round and said, 'I would like to know more about you if we are going to be friends. First of all, so there is no misunderstanding, you have a girlfriend, isn't that right?'

Leading question no mistake.

'Well . . . ' I went.

'No wells,' she got in quick. 'Absolutely no wells. You have a girlfriend or not?'

'Well . . . '

She started on the venomous again.

'Look Jane,' I went hasty, 'kind of hard to

answer you got to understand. Not very good manners in the bargain, sitting here with some totty, er excuse me Jane I mean some bird . . . some young lady and you start on about some other young lady only see . . . ' I was gabbing. She was casual. I started again. 'Well like Jane,' I went, 'there's that Kelly see like babymother, little Danny with her he's six see, only she gave me the elbow not long past, showed me the exit over some kraut footballer, just when I came out of nick like. Then again there's that Noreen, she's like fucking brilliant only . . . only . . . '

'Only what?' Her little beadies narrowed.

'Only she won't come across yet Jane you got to understand. She reckons I got to go straight first before she comes across. Then again now she might never come down my road again, seeing as how she got scarred up on my account, know what I mean?'

Her little beadies went a lot wider now.

'Nicky,' she went like my old head teacher.

'Miss . . . ' I went before I could stop.

'Nicky I think you have one or two things to fill in here, just a few episodes you left out of your life history man.'

She never let up that Jane. Real creamy bird you wanted to stay off the personals and maybe get on the sexy talk, only she wanted to be my friend and hear my business.

Noticed she never went on about whether she got a feller, only me and my birds.

'Er . . . ' I went for starters.

'You have told us quite honestly that you have been in prison Nicky, but unless I missed it I do believe you have not yet mentioned what it was for. Would you care to expand on that a little? A case of mistaken identity I expect?'

'It was an accident,' I went.

She howled.

Proper embarrassing you ask me. There you were making your case and she never took you serious. Birds I ask you. She kept on howling even had to wipe her jam pies. Surprising in that hotel they never came and did it for you.

'Tell me from the start Nicky my friend,' she went when she calmed down a bit. 'Tell me about your criminal career. Was this your first conviction then?'

'Er . . . not . . . not quite,' I goes. 'Sort of nearly . . . just sort of one or two before. Maybe if I been born fifteen years later . . . '

'I think you had better tell me from the start Nicky. First your crimes, then about Noreen, don't you think?'

Like I had a choice.

So I told her, sort of.

Gave her the gist on the offences, reckoned

they were sort of petty most of them. Mentioned the accident, why I spent a few years away. Then told her the story on Kelly and Noreen. Not so easy on what happened to Noreen. Been putting her slicing to the back of my mind while I was there, no point dwelling on it. Even when I met The Voice I tried not thinking on Noreen's scarring. Now it made me very very mean.

'They sliced her,' I went again. 'They sliced her on account of me. She got scarred for good.'

'Jesus.'

We were quiet.

'Jesus Nicky that's terrible.'

'Yeah.'

We drank our drinks.

'What are you going to do? How can you put it right with her? You better treat her good you know. This Noreen, you want her to be your girlfriend?'

'Yeah. She something special Jane. No reflection on you mind you're a classy bird and sort of nice looking . . . '

'Well thank you, but I understand she's even better?' She cackled.

'Not better Jane not better at all only . . . only . . . ' There I went and lost the place again.

'Only you love her?'

Jesus. Putting me through the ringer eh. Women.

'Only you love her?' she went again.

'Only, in a manner of speaking . . . '

She sat there waiting.

'Only I loves her, I suppose.'

There.

'Fuck me Jane,' I went, 'you don't half give a geezer a hard time innit? Dear oh law what you want, blood? Oh dear oh bleedin' dear.'

She stroked my mitt then kissed my cheek again, still made my teeth chatter. 'I think that's beautiful Nicky,' she went. 'Just beautiful. I hope I can meet Noreen some time. I'd like to be her friend. Meanwhile you will have to be very very nice to her.'

'I'll make her right Jane never you mind.'

'How?'

Thought about what I'd turn round and say. Thought about what she wanted to know.

Ah, fuck it then. 'I'm going to fuckin' kill 'em,' I went. 'Fuck 'em all, Jane, fuckin' fuck 'em all I'm going to shaft them no danger.'

She sat back. She never turned round and said anything a while.

We got another drink in silence.

Then she went 'Will that do any good Nicky do you think?'

Make me feel a lot better no problem.

I chewed on a bit of ice. She swirled round

her drink and sipped it a bit. We clocked a few people round the room a bit. Then she went 'Nicky now I know a bit more about you there's one more question I've got to ask you you know.'

I never felt like answering any more about Noreen just now. Might have guessed though it was going to be another stunner.

She put her little fingers on my shoulders then turned me round to face her. She gave it the big smile just for a sweetener, knew I could never resist that. Then she went for it.

'What do you really want out of life Nicky?' she turned round and went.

For definite I got an easier time up the interview room up Chingford nick. She did the relationships so now she wanted your brain, your future, your mum, all the stuff I got off the psychos back when I was a young offender. I had to holler.

Funny enough she never took any notice. Waited there till I finished. Seemed like she expected an answer.

So I had to give her answer. Fuck me, birds.

'Jesus Jane,' I went when she gave no mercy, 'fucked if I know, never really gave it no thought. Few birds few boozers, get a few bob in my pocket I spose same as most. Night out.' Jesus, what did most geezers want?

'You don't want to go back to prison?'

'Yeah you can take that for gospel Jane I don't want to go back in the nick yeah that's for starters.' That was one, keep her happy.

'And you want to be with Noreen?'

'Well yeah if she want me, never want to if she don't, fuck it then.'

'And you want your boy to grow up happy and strong?'

'Course.'

'And you want a job?'

'Job? Ain't many jobs round our way Jane. On account of how I'm in Jamaica looking for a bit of Uncle Bob. And help my mate out.'

'And you want to go down the pub and have a motor car and travel to France and Jamaica and other places?'

'Course, I ain't stupid you reckon Jane.'

'And you want to be happy?'

'Er . . . never really gave that a lot of thinking either Jane. All a bit heavy duty for me that, give you GBH of the brain. Better off just get up in the mornings, see what happens.'

'Hmmm,' she turned round and went.

We had a pause there.

Then she turned round and went 'Hmmm', again. She made it sound like now was when we started that world changing bit.

So I cackled at her. 'Jesus Jane,' I went,

'you giving me serious grief in my ears or what? You serious girl, you after changing my life innit? Birds, hell if I know, birds.'

Then we both burst out cackling together.

'I just think you ought to give it some consideration, that's all,' she went. 'Give it a bit of thought, which direction you want your life to go in.'

'I already told you I decided to go straight for that Noreen,' I went. 'How many more directions you want?'

'I will leave you to think about that my friend. Leave you to think about that.'

Jesus.

★   ★   ★

Two hours early I checked in the big bag, plonked it on the weigher while they did the business on my ticket.

'Mm, Mr Burkett, I do believe you are taking some coffee home,' went the bird with a sniff and her smile.

'You aren't wrong,' I went.

She took the bag through and the geezer at the back sniffed and went 'Ooh, smells like good coffee.'

I had about enough dosh left for a Mars Bar let alone duty free. Bought the *Gleaner* to settle down and wait an hour. Went outside the building for a wander and settled down by the shade with my carrier bags all full of coffee too.

One very smart geezer came and sat down beside me.

Oh boy.

'Yes man yes,' he went.

'No geezer no,' I went.

'Yes man. You travelling to Gatwick with me?'

'Travelling to Gatwick. Not with you friend unless you're the fucking pilot.'

'I just wondered. I am David.'

'Lucky you.' Never shook his mitt nor bumped his fist nor kissed him on both cheeks. I never wanted to know.

'I saw you counting your money man.'

Shit. Get in the airport and you lose your guard, first time in Jamaica I relaxed.

'I perceived you might be a bit short. Things can be bad when you spend all your savings on a holiday. You look to me like someone who works hard for a living, does not make a lot but would like a good time?'

Couldn't place his accent. Bit Jamaica, bit London bit Miami or some fucking place.

'So what's the bit of work?' I went.

'Well, I thought perhaps you would like to take a small package through for me to

England. You would be met at the other end, no problem.'

'A small package mate?'

'A small package yes man.'

'Bush tea for your auntie in Shepherd's Bush? Curry powder for your brother in Tottenham? Herbal medicine for the fuckin' ambassador?'

'Man I wouldn't insult you. Just half a pound of hash oil.'

'Just half a pound of hash oil.'

'Yeah man. Set you up when you get back. Nice money.'

'Nice dosh.'

'Nice dosh.'

'Fuckin' roll on,' I went. 'Fuckin' roll on, you security or what?'

'Security? No man, this genuine. I show you.'

'Fuckin' take it away smart boy. You reckon I came down off the fuckin' Christmas tree? Since when you made deals outside the airport? Deals happen up town man not under where the fuckin' cameras are rolling. And where's the real fuckin' deal eh? I get lifted here or Gatwick? You get on the fuckin' blower and take your slice off customs? And the real deal goes through nicely nicely? Fuckin' twenty pounds of hash oil or a bit of coke packed tight in some little suitcase while they all up watching me eh? Fuckin' fuck off out my sight man. You ain't got no class mister, take me for a fuckin' prick is all.'

I was upset. Me, I'm straight as a ruler.

More than that I never knew if he was a dealer or a set-up. I got up, went in the airport and straight in the toilets had a bleeding close look round. Pretty sure he never stuck it up my arse, first place they look. Not so sure he never stuck it in a pocket. Went round everything real careful. Seemed like all was clear.

So I went up Immigration.

'Mm, take some coffee home?' sniffed the pig.

'You aren't wrong,' I went.

Got through the bomb-checker, never showed up coffee.

'Good day,' went the geezer. 'Mm, I do believe you take some coffee home.'

'Correct.'

'Walk good,' he went.

I got in the door to the plane. 'Mm, I smell coffee,' goes the pilot, passing through at the time.

After dinner all the punters wanted coffee.

Then that plane took off again with me in it. None of the fuckers from Walthamstow were there, I took a good check in departures. Plenty of folk in there only none looked like cowboys out of Walthamstow.

There was hours of thinking on that plane. You started off in the evening and flew ten hours then you got in down Gatwick and it was fifteen hours later. Me there was no sense worrying, get on one end get off the other. They reckoned you slept on the overnight. Only I was plenty sure if I stopped concentrating that pilot sure to take a nosedive like kamikaze maybe and we'd be a submarine. Best I stayed awake. Any event it paid off we got there.

Up Gatwick it never seemed worth troubling the boys in the red channel for a few beans of coffee. Might be legal for all I reckoned. Got just a bottle of rum so went through the green. 'Mm, coffee smells good,' went the pig. I gave a little cackle like they expected. Went through on the nod.

Got on the slow train to London. Fast one costs the price of your air ticket. Three separate companies charge you three separate prices Gatwick to London, got to make sense to someone. Me I got on the cheap one the same as everyone else then bunked the tube.

'Do I smell coffee?' went some geezer on the train up from Brighton in a suit.

'Dunno mate do you smell coffee?' I goes.

'Mm.'

I reckoned I had half a grand of coffee in there. Do for me.

When I got back up my gaff I made a proper cup of tea. Tea's fucking terrible abroad.

# 12

Good to get back in England. Good to get back in Walthamstow any road. Not only they understood what you said in Walthamstow, you got a pint of lager and some ganja and a decent Jamaican pattie any time you wanted. Except the airport no geezer ever offered that ganja up Jamaica. Patties they all got goat in them.

Hotter up Jamaica though got to say. Got more hummingbirds than Walthamstow in the bargain and all that rain forest. Still Walthamstow got Lloyd Park and the ducks.

I was glad to be back know what I mean.

Up my gaff the heating was on. Got to be Sharon came round, no-one else got a key not even that Noreen. She was a good'un that Sharon. And pint of milk in the fridge and loaf of bread and some butter. I made six rounds thick toast and wedged the butter. Four cups real tea. Went to bed.

Got up again two hours later, either I was totalled or I felt sonic, couldn't decide. Walked once round the flat and yes I was totalled. Needed a pick-me-up. Place was full of coffee only it was all in beans no use to me.

Found a couple of Es back of the fridge ought to do the trick.

Belled George the warrant. Got him at home.

'George mate,' I goes, 'how your bruises mate?'

'Jesus,' he goes. 'I changed my home number and you still got it.'

Start again.

'George mate,' I goes, 'how your bruises mate?'

'Fair to middling,' he goes. 'Hope to be back at work next week. How about yours Nicky and them broken fingers. You been convalescing round your mum's or what?'

'No George, I popped over Jamaica mate.'

'Jamaica!'

'Yeah, convalescing like you turned round and said, reckoned it might help George, bit of sunshine you know, ought to try it. Just got back matter of fact.'

'You thieving little bastard!'

'Now George that ain't very friendly. Try to keep mellow now.'

'All out of your discharge grant I suppose. Or the dole.'

'Came out of savings George since you ask.'

'Savings my arse. Next time you get a fine up the court Nicky I shall want it all out of your savings or bang you up straight off no messing.'

'I'm a reformed character George. I got that rehabilitation you heard about it?'

'I think I just saw a pig flying past Nicky.'

'Anyway George very nice to chatter with you mate only I want to do business like.'

'Nicky. Just you wait a minute while my blood pressure calms down.' He put the receiver down while he walked round got a cup of tea and came back. All on my phone bill.

'Nicky what you on about?'

'George I got heavy news up Jamaica on why we got mash up, you hear what I'm saying?'

'Nicky . . . Nicky, you got information you go up Chingford and talk to TT. Only you don't gas over the phone, you hear me?'

'You trying to tell me them bastard Bill got me tapped?'

'All kinds of technology these days Nicky, and all kinds of people. In the bargain I don't want to be involved. I got involved before, see where it got me.'

'Need a talking George.'

'You have a talking with TT and see what he's got to say.'

'George I hate that fucker he's fucking CID you hear what I'm saying?'

'And I'm a police officer too. You want to speak to the police you do it official.'

Dear oh dear. Everything was official these days. Remembered the time you were short of readies Friday afternoon you went round the copshop grassed up a few villains. Monday morning you got your payback off the Regional. Not me you understand only grasses.

I belled Rameez on his mobile. He was unobtainable.

Unobtainable? Maybe he was shafting some bird, meant he was unobtainable ten minutes. Tried again fifteen minutes later, gave him five minutes in case they did it twice. Still unobtainable. How could he do business? How could he keep in touch? Never still in hospital. I rang him at home, got one of his tasty sisters. She turned round and said he was unobtainable.

Belled Sharon on my old mobile I gave her.

'Customer Comfort,' she went.

What?

'What?' I goes.

'Customer Comfort here how can I help you do you wish to make a booking?'

'Sharon what the fuck's this?'

'Oh, all right Nicky?'

'You never answered what I turned round and said Sharon. What the fuck's this

Customer Whosit?'

'Visiting massage Nicky.'

'Visiting what?'

'Visiting massage. Never told you yet, reckoned one of the girls give you a surprise visit one day. Only we set up a visiting massage business, like a pizza you know home delivery.'

Jesus.

'Jesus,' I went. 'Things moved on Sharon while I was away. You one of them birds visiting?'

'Not me Nicky. Me I'm the radio controller like on the minicabs you know. Shelley Rosario she set it up local and one or two of the lads, know what I mean?'

'Which of them lads?'

'Sherry McAllister and Wayne Sapsford and Marty Fisherman does the driving.'

'In a Merc?'

She giggled. Marty always known like Mercedes Marty on account of he lifted a Merc the one time. Could be Audi Marty or Astra Marty or Sierra Marty or that matter Lada Marty on account of he lifted everything on wheels, only Mercedes Marty stuck. Drove that Merc round the estate pleased as a fart till the Bill lifted him ten minutes later seeing it was unusual clocking a fifteen-year-old driving a Mercedes on Priory Court.

'And who behind it?'

'Me I'm only the controller Nicky, send the girls out and them minders stay in the motors waiting. Don't know who's the guvnor.'

It fitted in. Sharon never knew nish about it only it fitted in. It was never on account of she was my sister she got warned. Coincidence only. She got warned on account of her mates were setting up a business and she was the front. Setting up a business stepping on a few toes. Old days you never got working girls round Walthamstow, you got to go up the Cross for a massage. These days there was more around, singles and syndicates both.

Sharon was the face, the operator. Never mind who was the power, she got the warning.

'Sharon where's that Rameez? Need a talking urgent.'

'By his uncle up Birmingham Nicky a week. Secret. Out the way.'

'Tell him bell me about a meeting.'

'I tell him Nicky. You all right? You come round give us the news on your holidays eh? Or I come round your place?'

'Best I come round Sharon see Mum. Shithead around?'

'Late shift.'

'Come round tomorrow. Oh, and I reckon

it was you looked after my gaff when I was away innit?'

'Leave it out Nicky, no problem.'

'See you.' We all needed that talking. I got to speak to that TT about it.

* * *

'Gimme TT,' I went when they put me through the CID up Chingford.

'He's out,' they turned round and said.

'Where's he at?'

'Officer TT is on an observation. Who is it anyway?'

'Tell him Nicky wants him urgent.'

Five minutes later he was on. His observation got to be up the toilet.

'Nicky.'

'TT.'

'Nicky I heard you were in Jamaica. What you got for me? Brought me some of that ganja eh?'

So he soon heard I was up Jamaica.

'Need a talking. You and me and some more.'

'Go on Nicky.'

'Need it urgent. Before we all get stitched up goodstyle.'

'You want to give me some idea what you're saying here?'

'Nah. All I'm saying is we got to have a big talking, see what the score is. Then next what I want to hear is, are you on the level geezer? Tell you for nothing, what we're talking here is bent coppers so what I want is where you're standing, are you straight or what?' Seemed like the best way to find out whether he was on the graft was like ask him.

He wasn't impressed. 'EXCUSE ME HERE! What the fuck are you talking about? I'm a police officer.'

'Don't make me crack up. I want witnesses here and I got to have the Old Bill, only Old Bill not covered in shit. Get George Marshall in there for a start, know he's legit.'

'You little bastard what the fuck are you — '

'Cut it out geezer.' I was in no mood these days. 'Get George there and then you bring one other pig you reckon ain't bent, I want someone so straight they never even got a hair curl.'

'I'll bring Karen Mohammed. Mind you I totally reject any suggestion — '

'Yeah yeah. I got to bring a crowd, already involved or got to be involved soon. That safe with you?'

'Of course it's safe only . . . '

'And I reckon I get someone off the Council got a bit of saw.'

'The Council!'

'Yeah and maybe some bird off the paper.'

'What the fuck is this you little bastard?'

'Just cover my back is all, and they got tasty little birds on that paper. Then again I maybe get my probation down.' I was giving it brain cells, cover that angle too.

'Probation! About as much use as a wet weekend.'

'Yeah I'll get that Andy, get him off sitting by his house making that homebrew when he goes home. Got to warn you mate don't you ever touch that homebrew you get offered. Went round his one day gave me a cupful. Twenty minutes and I reckoned I was a green monster.'

We had a pause in the conversation.

'I won't ask what this is all about,' he went. 'It had better be good is all. Where are we going to have this famous meeting then?' Now we clocked his little game for sure. The one hand he reckoned I sucked big ones, the other hand I might have big news week for him here and he eyeballed that promotion coming on, no more shift work and man-size expenses.

'Whipps Cross canteen,' I turned round and said.

'What?'

They never sold beer up Whipps Cross

canteen, not such a help for a meeting. On the other hand fit in with all our outpatients and physio appointments though. Me I was there most days since I got out of the ward except when I was up Jamaica, and since Jamaica I needed even more. And George and Rameez and Dean still got a need for that physio no danger. Served mean chips in that canteen too. Maybe they wanted purchase a bit of Blue Mountain coffee for afters, who knows.

'And you get this Karen bird and then you never give out a fucking whisper, not no-one at all you get my meaning? This is serious mischief here if I got it stacked right. Wrong geezers get the message and we're buried you and me both.'

'I hear what you're saying Nicky only this is most irregular and if anything — '

'Whipps Cross canteen four o'clock Monday.' I was out of there.

⋆   ⋆   ⋆

Next I belled that Andy up Probation, only he was never in.

'Nicky where you been?' went Rosie on reception. 'You missed two appointments Nicky and Andy he's on a week off doing his decorating and that Annabel Higgs I heard her say something about warrants and courts and that.'

'Jesus Rosie you're giving me GBH of the earhole here. I only rang up for a natter with that Andy.'

'Only you're on licence Nicky ain't you? You got to report. Here I saw your mum down the market on Friday, don't she look well since she had the op?'

'Rosie this is brain damage here. Telling me I missed two appointments?'

'Two appointments Nicky in succession.'

'And that Andy's off.' I knew enough not to mention even Rosie about how I was round Jamaica. In the rush forgot to inform Probation I was off up Jamaica on parole.

'Who's on office duty today?'

'Let me see, Dorothy Makerere.'

'She all right?'

'She a kind lady. Won't grass you up. Dresses nice too.'

'Tell her I'll pop in later eh?'

'I'll tell her. Don't you let me down now.'

'No problem.' Fuck me another call to make.

So I got Andy at home, do him a favour get him off the decorating.

'Jesus Nicky I changed my number once to stop you ringing me here.' They all changed their numbers it looked like, seemed to reckon it did the trick. 'How in hell did you get it?'

'Hardly worth the trouble changing you ask me Andy. Anyway seeing as how you invited me round your gaff that one time, you forgot how you wanted me picking up that bent stereo and teach the kids how to steal a motor?'

He had to cackle. Did go round his one time he gave me an old bed for that Kelly when she got her flat. Not so likely he dealt stereos and the kids were about four years old. Still I offered.

'Well, what is it Nicky anyway? I was making quite good progress on the kitchen till you rang. Now it's a two-day setback while I get over you winding me up. Still, go ahead please, won't you?'

'Andy you got to be in the canteen at Whipps Cross Monday four o'clock.'

'I see. Any special reason? They've got lasagne on the menu?'

'Can't turn round and tell you Andy. Only don't be letting on to no-one right? Especially not no-one out your office. This one for me Andy eh?'

Then I rang off.

When I belled the paper I remembered that nice bit of stuff wrote me up after the post office. Asked for her.

'Hello,' she came on, 'this is Bridget Tansley, how can I help you?' Sounded like I got some finance company or the bailiff where they all talked like that.

'You the bird wrote me up after that post office?'

'Excuse me, I don't think I've got you yet. You are . . . ?'

'Nicky Burkett. You reckon you did that bit on the post office up Wood St?'

'Oh . . . yes. Nicky Burkett! I remember you, yes. Twenty-three, just came out of prison, a bit mouthy, that's you?'

'You got it. Now you want a big story?'

'Like I want to eat. What have you got for me?'

'Can't turn round and tell you yet. You meet me in Jimmy's on Markhouse Rd three o'clock Monday. All right?' Wanted some witnesses soon, never wanted the word getting round too early.

'Yes . . . what's Jimmy's?'

'Dear oh law, Jimmy's is only the best café in Walthamstow. English or Thai what you fancy.'

'Oh I'm sorry I don't know Walthamstow that well yet, this is my first job you see and that post office story was my best one so far.'

'Pity you made up the half of it then.'

'I come from Bishop's Stortford you see.'

'Say no more. You be there Monday then?'
'I'll be there.'

Then I got to work on the rest now I got the insurance. No problem getting my mates there. Problem was staying out the way making sure there was no aggravation any sort until Monday. Nothing to fuck up the plans.

★   ★   ★

I went up Wandsworth to see that Slip. Went on the tube this time took half the fucking day. Then had to wait nearly an hour while they found him in the nick. Me I wasn't in the best of humours by then.

No holding him back though.

'My man!' he goes.

'Fuck me Slip where the fuck you been man, humping the governor's missis or what?'

'Normal location man, normal location, sweeping and mopping that wing, I do believe that the finest smartest wing corridor in the whole of the British prison system since I got my little hands on it. Sweeping and mopping man, sweeping and mopping.'

He was a caution that Slip you had to grant it.

'I belled my grannie!' he went.

'You what?'

'I belled my grannie. She say you a fine young man and I got nice friends. Hoo! I tell her you a leading vill-ain she want to be careful you never tiefed her sweet potatoes.'

'Listen up here Slip, I paying my taxes for you to make them transatlantic phone calls?'

'What taxes is them? Anyways I no depend on no system man, I pays by free enterprise that little weed you brought me that went a nice way round the prison you know. And purchased myself a number of them little green phonecards with which I belled my grannie.'

'She some lady your grannie eh?'

'Ain't that the truth? And she say she hear you went up them mountains did the business them small small farmers. That a fact? Nicky we in business here? Things is sweet?'

'She heard any more like any small problems?'

'She ain't sure only she heard some rumour you finished up grievous in some village after you came down that mountain too quick? That the truth brother? You such a big man you don't need no path you try to fly down that mountain?'

I leaned over that table. 'You want Twix or Mars Bars?' I went. 'And them apples and all?'

'Twix and the usual. Just fill up that tray man.'

'We ain't got only half an hour Slip so maybe I get you the stuff then give you the story straight off. It ain't no short one.'

'Maybe you like to come back in my cell and give me that history. Get free board you like.'

I went up the WVS. Then I gave him the whole story. Gave him the whole thing beginning to end in the time. Sometimes he was happy like an angel, sometimes he was clumped almost like I never put sugar in his tea.

He was gutted about the deckchairs.

'You sure bro?' he went. 'You fuckin' sure? They got deckchairs already not just them loungers?'

'I sure. Fuck knows why maybe out of some antique shop but they got deckchairs. Deckchairs is available. Jamaica heard of deckchairs.'

'Fuckin' shit me man, this is heavy duty disappointment, some tiefing entrepreneur got there first it would appear.'

'What was that word Slip?'

'Tiefing?'

'Familiar with that one. Next one.'

'Entrepreneur. Tell me it French fatso so you got to understand it.'

'Just on account of I did French never means I knows all the words. I heard it though. Never mind the meaning so they got one of them bastards up Jamaica you reckon? Secret?'

'Yeah one of them tiefing entrepreneurs got there first, got to be. Tiefed my idea. Took them deckchairs. Hot damn! Now we got to think up some other scheme then bro innit?'

He was upset. No denying it he was upset. Looked like he might pass away there and then out of that disappointment.

Let him drink his tea then his coffee then eat his Twix and apples and crisps and biscuits. Let all that settle. Then I went 'Only we still got to think of something else? That coffee ain't enough it works?'

'That coffee brilliant man fuckin' brilliant. No problem there at all at all. Only for the perfect enterprise, you dig, it got to have products going in both directions at once. You never send a ship out empty to that Carib Sea for getting them bananas innit? You send out them things them Caribs need, like . . . computers and . . . '

'Deckchairs.'

'Shut the fuck up Nicky.'

We sat and thought on this a bit. Then we sat and thought some more. Then it was the end of the visit and we still never got a useful thought.

'We think about it more,' he went. 'We still make a profit Nicky maybe on that coffee only you understand we got to maximise our investment.'

'Yeah. Got to.'

'Maximise that fuckin' investment man! Now you think hard on it brother, and meanwhile you go up that British Overseas Trade Board like I told you, enquire about a licence, you got me?'

'I got you. You still be here?'

'Fuckin' Highpoint next time the transport goes they reckon. I see you there man.'

'No problem.'

Only then events got in the way again.

# 13

Monday four o'clock they were all there. Andy off Probation five minutes late like always. We took up one side the canteen, put all the tables together. I already met that Bridget up Jimmy's, put her in the picture and brought her along.

TT reckoned he ought to take charge. 'Now Nicky,' he went loud when we all got our tea, 'you want to tell us what this is all about? This is most improper my even being here, so . . . '

'Shut the fuck up copper,' goes Jimmy Foley.

'Shut the fuck up copper,' goes the rest.

That Karen Mohammed though was a bit of a looker. Still tell she was Old Bill from the way she walked, only she got a sharp body. Straight hair too like he promised.

There was George the warrant never wanted to be there. Next to him was Jimmy Foley and Dean Longmore. Tina Duffy was there who I screwed when I was fifteen only now she was with Sherry McAllister sat next to her. Paulette James took a break in training, went to school with her only now she was running for England. Shelley Rosario. Sharon was there, never liked bringing Sharon in only this time no choice. Kept Noreen out of it. Rameez was there still looked like shit brought Aftab and Afzal and Javed with him his minders. Out of the Housing I got Junior Merrill was in our pool team, wanted someone off the Council. He took some flexi-time, never knew what the fuck was going down but still came. Then a few mates came along for numbers and never wanted to be missed out, Darren Boardman and Elvis Littlejohn and Wayne Sapsford and Marty Fisherman. Not short of car thieves case one was needed. Not short of anything.

'Now you all shut the fuck up!' I went. No other way I knew to start a talking.

'Yeah, shut the fuck up,' they all went, least my mates did. Others bottled it like used the tact.

'We got a long talking to do,' I turned round and said.

Sipped my tea. Never knew what to turn round and say next.

'Tell it Nicky tell it!' went Paulette, hyped up now like it was an international.

'All right!' I went hyped up in the bargain. Then I was away. 'I got to tell it from the start,' I goes suddenly soft. 'Then you all tell me what the fuck we do next.

'All started,' I went, 'when fucking Old Bill wanted me to do some errands.'

'Who me?' went George. 'I'm the effing Old Bill is that it?'

'Nah Nicky,' went Rameez. 'Nah Nicky, started before then, I was already up Whipps Cross by then remember?'

'Listen up!' I went.

'Let him tell it,' went that Elvis. 'Tell it like the way it was, brother, tell it!' Brought up in the congregation that Elvis.

So I started out again. 'Listen up!' I goes. 'I tell it from the start the way I seen it, know what I mean? Then you all can get in after, all right? All get a spot, like Rameez and the Bill and Jimmy and Sharon and the rest you all say what happen. Hear what I'm saying?

'Awright. Here we go. So it all started when I got out of nick came out the Central got leaned on by the Old Bill. I never wanted no aggravation got a good attitude. Going after some of that rehabilitation.'

So I told it. Told it from the start. Left out a few bits like that Noreen coming round my gaff, not part of the story. Left out about that Jane in the bargain, never wanted grief off Noreen after it got back, even though there was never any action. Left out how much coffee I brought back. Told them what they got to know.

Time I finished there was old biddies listening up came in for a cup after their cancer appointments. Counter staff coming round for an earwig pretending to be cleaning up. Security passing by reckoned they'd take their break now. Fortunate none of them understood the situation I hoped, reckoned it was some film script maybe. I was mega round there.

Finished and they all gave it applause, seven out of ten on the clapometer. Geezers whistled.

I got another cup of tea and a scone. No-one else wanted to go next I was such a star.

Then TT had to do it. He got up to speak. All groaned and spat.

'Maybe it would be helpful,' he went like he was talking to some school class, 'if I was to give you some repetition background here.'

'You can fuck off into the background you want,' went that Shelley. Never got on that well with the Bill did Shelley.

'Tell you how we got involved — the police — in all of this,' he carried on. That Karen nodded along for supporting him and when she did the nodding you could clock everything bobbing up and down, she got a sharp body especially being out of uniform. First time I ever wanted to give it to a pig.

Quite lost my attention for a moment.

'We had had our suspicions for a long time about stolen motors,' he went. 'New motors, high performance, probably going straight out of the country. Now we appreciate that this is all strictly off the record, I am taking you into my confidence here because of the nature of this business and it must go no further right?'

Everyone howled. George choked on his tea. Knew the score George. News got to be round the manor about twenty minutes after we left Whipps Cross, next day everyone in the borough heard, except the enemy we hoped.

Carried on regardless that TT. 'And we had our suspicions about Mickey Cousins, only I'm telling you now he's a big man and got powerful connections so we had to tread softly. So we mounted a surveillance operation.'

Big fucking deal.

'And I was part of that operation,' he went modestly, 'only DS Grant was a bigger part.' DS fucking Grant to you and me. 'Then one night when DS Grant was surveilling, he happened to observe our friend Rameez, we believe, pursuing an altercation with one Mickey Cousins.'

'Reckon that was what I was doing then,'

goes Rameez, 'pursuing an altercation.'

'Pursuing an altercation,' went Aftab and Afzal.

'What that in Urdu?' went Javed.

'So we believe DS Grant intervened in order to extricate Rameez, who was by then unconscious, from the situation. Only then sadly DS Grant was overcome.'

'Bought it,' went Jimmy.

'Blown away,' went Dean.

'Wasted,' went Darren.

'And of course we have absolutely no evidence at this stage that Mickey Cousins or his mates were even there, except for the possible testimony of Rameez here. And the next part is highly secret I'm afraid, since we cannot reveal our plans for an arrest lest it should be counter-productive. Isn't that right Rameez?'

'Ought to left me alone,' goes Rameez. 'Situation under control I was about to make a comeback. Guys were well out of order though. And yeah I ain't made no statement yet, that what you mean to say?'

'What happen man?' they all went. 'You can tell us man!' Rameez never made no statement so far on account of he preferred being alive he reckoned.

Only now he told his bit like he told me up the ward first time.

When he finished they gave him applause polite like, only never applause like I got. See too many scars on him. Funny how now he got the scars some of the mental went out of Rameez, like he was almost normal. Still never wanted him digging me out though never wanted any slicing contest thank you. Only he was quiet now.

Then they all went round everyone. George did his bit. Sharon and Jimmy and Dean went how they got warned or more. We all listened up, everyone put up their stories. It was all coming together in the frame now just like I clocked it.

Only by this time I had eight cups of their tea. Whipps Cross afford to build another hospital on our profits. Anyway by now I was wanting to get pissed up.

'See here,' I went, 'we got to make plans innit? Only I need a pint of lager first, know what I mean?'

'Boozer,' went all my mates. 'Down the boozer.' Pigs never argued, most of CID always half cut on duty anyway. Junior out of Housing still never knew what the fuck he was doing there. Andy looking at his watch wondering about putting his kids to bed probably.

Then TT made his first popular announcement.

'Reckon the first round's on the firm!' he went. 'Funds can stand one round I expect, but one round only!'

Not such a bad geezer that TT after all, got a touch on that one got a result there.

So we went up the Alfred Hitchcock, where the style was you sat very quiet and gazed out over the forest.

* * *

'Fuck 'em,' went Karen Mohammed, spoke for the first time now she got a lager inside her. 'I say fuck 'em from here to Canvey and back.'

And she was the straight one.

'Rump 'em,' goes TT banging his fist on the table. Couple of Scotches and he was anybody's. 'Rump 'em in the morning, rump 'em in the afternoon, rump 'em all night, show 'em there's no messing with Chingford eh.'

There was a deal of banging and cackling.

'Now hold on up,' goes George then, 'now let's see a bit of calm here please let's deal with this natural. God knows I don't want to be in this at all, it's most irregular, but let's see how we can do this by the book eh, or at least some of it by the book. Authorised. Proper. Only first let's see what we got before we start on this silly talk. So where do we head from, what's the situation we begin with?'

He was good as gold that George you got to say. Matters were getting out of hand here, brought it back into control.

'We got a conspiracy,' he carried on and said.

'We heard what Nicky worked out when he was doing that thinking in Jamaica. First of all it was Rameez, who they reckoned was stepping on their territory. DS Grant got into it by accident so they murdered him, murdered a copper I'm very sorry to say.

'Then Nicky walked into that post office raid and they thought he did it deliberate. Then they put my name up for spiking their plans because they thought I pointed him up that way.

'Around then it looked to everyone like Nicky was the connection. Even later it still looked that way because all the people got warned seemed to know Nicky. But the way I look at it, which is the way we heard Nicky looks at it, that ain't the truth of the matter.

'The real connection is, everyone Nicky knows is a tealeaf.'

Thank you George my warrant officer.

'Pure coincidence,' he went on, 'pure coincidence that all the people we're talking about here are known to Nicky Burkett. The real situation is the other way round. Might be plenty of others got warned for all we know, only Nicky doesn't know them. All we know is that a heap of people got warned. Since they were all villains, there was a fair chance they were known to Nicky Burkett.'

Bit hard on my rep I reckoned that George. Noreen was never a tealeaf, nor her mum and dad. My mum was never a tealeaf for that matter. But I let all go.

'And you, George?' I went. 'And you got a whacking?'

He ignored me, so far in his stride he was never being put off by some minor interruption in his theory. 'So Jimmy got warned,' he went on, 'and Sharon and probably lots more as well as the people they put in the hospital. So they probably thought they'd done the business, put enough fear out. But then, just as if to add insult to it, they heard Nicky was going out to Jamaica! Probably their best import area! Stepping on their toes was never in it, this was stuffing it right down their throat to their belly button.'

'Taking the right piss,' went Dean.

'So they decided they had to go in heavy. Never mind the risks they took on being exposed, maybe they panicked, who knows. They decided they had to deal with this once and for all, give a lesson in manners to anyone who needed to listen.'

'Get it sorted proper.'

'Give out the message on the airwaves.'

'But then,' George went on like the preacher, 'what happened but Nicky got away.' Pause for effect. 'So now we have to ask ourselves this question — what comes next?'

'Tell it George!'

'Chill out man!' Geezers encouraged him on.

'Why is it none of us saw all this happen? Why is it we never heard about it in the borough?

'I've been thinking I can tell you. And I decided there can only be one reason.' He waited for effect. 'It's got to be because not only is there plenty more people who got warned, there's plenty more people involved in the conspiracy. People we never even heard of yet, not only involved in the plot but involved in keeping it from the rest of us. What we heard so far I reckon is only the tip of the iceberg.

'So before we hit them official, police like, before we take out the action we got to find out who else is involved, why we never heard about it, who's been giving it the hush.'

'Yeah man!'

'Give it to us George! Show us the way man!'

Then there was another pause. A pause for thinking and drinking. And when you thought about it, you saw you got to make him right.

'Thank you,' he goes gratified to one and all, suddenly the leader here. 'Thank you. So I suggest we make some plans.'

*   *   *

'First,' he went on, 'I suggest to get the wider picture we need to start a bit of unofficial surveillance here. Not only the police maybe haven't got the resources for all this, frankly they aren't going to believe us anyway. And then again, we might be surveilling the police.'

Jesus. There got to be mushrooms in that beer.

'Anyway we want it kept very quiet, except half the petty villains in the borough know it already because you're all here. So I suggest we use the next week, till everyone else knows about it, getting you lot of . . . tosspots and plonkers to do a bit of quiet observation for us on the side. And that means me too! Then during the week we get properly set up with the police so if the information comes in we can intervene officially from the top. Is that all right with you lot? And you TT?'

We were stunned.

We were gobsmacked.

That TT his brain just fell out his arse.

Only goes to show you never can tell.

'George! George!'

'Tell it out for George now!'

He heard all that before so he wasn't so impressed this time.

All we knew was there was three fuckers went out to Jamaica. They got to have allies, they got to have troops, but there was no way to start out except with them. There was Mickey Cousins warned me on the street even before Jamaica and probably sorted out DS fucking Grant. There was that Annabel Higgs off Probation not only came out Jamaica but threatened on getting me recalled to nick for missing a couple of poxy appointments. Then there was that Chief Superintendent Armitage. Got to be powerful, maybe knew where all the work was to be done.

Oh, and he happened to get Noreen sliced all down her cheek with a Stanley knife. Well well.

We had plenty bodies available. We got to be able to watch a few bastard fuckers for a week. Only question was who was best for it.

I looked at George. George looked at me.

'We got to follow them round like George turned round and said,' I goes. 'We got to know every little thing about them fuckers.'

'Fuckers,' they all went.

'Only remember they been clocking some of us for damage with intent. So you got to be careful they ain't clocking you same time you clocking them.'

'Right.'

'Morning noon and night we got to clock 'em.'

'Yo!'

'TT you sort out a bug on their phones know what I mean?'

Even pissed up he had to snort on that one. 'Do me a favour fuck's sake,' he went, 'they got to be authorised personal by God them buggings. Easier to get a meal for two on expenses than a listen on someone's phone.'

What he wanted us to hear anyway. No-one credited it and even that Karen Mohammed rolled up her mince pies, still there was nothing we could touch on that one. He got an attitude so he got an attitude.

'Maybe you can make a few vehicles available then,' I went. Just winding him up.

But we got to make serious plans.

★   ★   ★

First off we needed someone legit on Mickey Cousins. Someone quick and legit, he never knew as villains.

'Elvis and Paulette,' I went.

'Eh?'

'Elvis, you the sharpest geezer around.'

'You right.' Elvis got his Raybans, his luminous trainers, his old BMW, his karate certificates, he was a cool dude.

'Paulette you can run quick.'

'Hope to tell.'

'You both take a bit of time off? Elvis from pulling them chicks, Paulette from that running for England?'

'Fit it in around my training,' went Paulette. She gave up her job for that running anyway when she won some meet in Switzerland or some place netted her a ton.

'Elvis?'

'Be hard. Have to fit it in around my training too.'

'Safe. Now you know where this geezer got his gaff?'

'Somewhere up the forest?' went Elvis, found the forest useful time to time.

'Yeah and you know where his yard is?'

'Everyone knows.'

'Right. So you two got to be our eyes. Clock who he meets, where he goes, when he gets there, what he has for his dinner eh?'

'Fuck matters what he has for dinner?' goes Jimmy Foley.

'Report back here same time next week?' I goes.

'I'd prefer the Whipps Cross canteen,' goes that Karen Mohammed. 'When I get a lager inside me I start to get a bit aggressive I'm afraid.'

Aggressive. I let my little beadies wander up and down her a bit. Maybe I got a thing about uniforms. Except she was CID so she never wore one. Probably got one at home though.

'What about that Armitage then?' I goes, an excuse for clocking her instead of that TT.

Only he jumped in. 'I don't know where to start,' he went, even though he just started. 'I never heard anything like it. Don't have any doubts about it, I make you right only I never heard anything like it.' He put his bonce in his mitts and shook it. 'This whole situation makes me wonder about everything.'

'Fucking brace up copper,' went Dean.

'Fucking brace up copper,' went Jimmy.

'Yeah brace up man,' went Aftab and Afzal.

'You want to clock him?' I goes to Karen. 'He got a feel for the birds?'

'I wouldn't know but I don't think it's a very good idea I'm afraid. I'm not sure if he knows me personally but I'm quite sure he would recognise me.'

Recognise, yeah, I reckoned I might recognise them too.

'Rameez?' I went.

'You got me bro. You got me.'

So Rameez and his buddies took on Armitage.

That just left Annabel Higgs.

'George?' I went.

'Eh?'

It was perfect. George worked down the courts, no-one ever knew where he got to anyway. Keep one eye on his punters and one on that Higgs. No danger hardly refuse. We never even discussed it. That Andy my probation was near wetting himself in the background thinking about his boss being clocked by the pigs, still no problem there.

So we booked another meet the next week. Meanwhile we sorted how they all could give me the word on what was happening. Do a bit of preparation like before we came together again for the big plan.

'Oh and by the way,' went TT, recovered a bit now, 'these are very mean people you know behind this, if this is all how we see it. Find out you're tailing them and someone might not be impressed, not at all. Might even reckon you're taking the piss. Remember what happened before. So you watch yourselves, eh.'

George and Karen like the good pigs, they played round in their beer a bit embarrassed. The rest just cackled. No need to remind Rameez they might not be very impressed on seeing him.

# 14

'Can you feel my cervix then Nicky?' went Noreen.

'Say what?'

'Like can you feel my cervix eh? You know where it is?'

'Never know what you got up there Noreen. Feels much the same as usual I reckon.'

'Never mind what your other birds felt like. You got to be able to feel my cervix, make sure it's in proper.'

'Your cervix in proper?'

'Don't be such a bleeding fool Nicky, course my cervix is in proper. Make sure the diaphragm's in proper. If it is you should be able to feel my cervix right.'

'Oh.'

'Can you feel it?'

I had to pause then.

'What's it feel like Noreen?'

'God give me patience,' she went. 'Good job we don't depend on men. Draw you a map, eh? Here, get out the way a minute and let me have a feel.' She pushed me off her and did a bit of work. 'Yeah, seems to be OK. All right then Nicky, let's get back on the job shall we, don't keep a girl waiting?' Then she giggled.

Jesus. First off when she turned round and said she made love with a cap I reckoned she meant some baseball cap. Then she goes how she gets ready in the bathroom so I thought maybe it was a shower cap. Seemed a bit kinky, still I heard some geezers never took their socks off so she was entitled to her opinions, wear whatever she wanted. Then she explained it went inside her. Not enough room for a baseball cap.

Taken me several years getting Noreen to here. Then it seemed like when it happened she made all the moves.

She put a note through my door going *Nicky I'm free on Saturday night. I will come round at nine o'clock. Give me a bell if you can't make it, otherwise I will be here.*

Nine o'clock sharp on Saturday she was banging on the door. Least she was giving it little knocks like birds do.

I went down and let her in.

'Fuck me Noreen that's a beautiful bottle of Bacardi you got there,' I went. 'And you ain't all that bad yourself come to think of it.'

'Get your bum in that flat and stop winding me up before I beat your brains,' she went. 'If you got any.' We went upstairs.

'Noreen,' I went as we got upstairs, 'I hope you ain't eaten yet?'

'Matter of fact no Nicky, thought we'd order a takeaway, what you say?'

'I made us some nosh.'

'You never. Mean to tell me you heard about treating a girl nice?'

'Got to treat a bird a bit special now and again keep 'em sweet,' I went. 'Give them their spends let 'em go shopping make 'em feel appreciated else they go off with a next man, know what I mean?'

'Such a romantic Nicky you ought to be in a Barbara Cartland. So what have you got eh?'

I made plantains and green bananas and sweet potatoes and ackees and callaloo all with a gravy and dumplings like I had in Jamaica. Solid meal. Started to go down real good with that Bacardi and orange juice and ice. Put some sounds on and we got real mellow.

'You been by Mrs Shillingford today?' I went. Being Saturday when Noreen was starting to make a habit going round there.

'Yes and she say you come round tomorrow for dinner if you've been a good boy.' I went round for dinner Sundays by Mrs Shillingford's any week I never committed a crime. Standing arrangement before I went in the nick, so now we carried on afterwards. She asked me and I told her when I belled her Saturdays.

'You tell her I'd been a good boy?'

'I told her I would know about it after tonight.'

Jesus, what was she saying here? First hint I got she might be planning the business for the night. Only first she went round discussed it with Mrs Shillingford! Women.

'Maybe you put out a broadcast Noreen?'

She never answered that one. Only came a bit closer on the settee.

'So have you been a good boy Nicky?'

'How you mean?'

'You know what I mean. Have you been committing any of them crimes? You know if you never commit any crimes I might think about giving you a bit of nookie, you remember that?'

Christ. Not something likely to escape a geezer's mind.

'Noreen I ain't never done nothing. Even I wanted to I got injuries all over never let me.'

'Mm. And you know you better not either in the future.'

Seemed like I passed that test. So I tried it on, cuddled up to her on that settee, put one arm round her shoulders the other up her skirt like you do. She felt like she was hot and in the mood.

Then she went sudden: 'And you got the result of that test Nicky?'

No, not the same test.

Jesus what a passion killer. No end to what you got to do these days.

'Oh, er, yeah I reckon I did Noreen.'

'And?'

'And what?'

'You know and what, so you can stop winding me up before I get serious vex with you Nicky.'

'Let me see,' I went, 'not too sure I remember Noreen. Either positive or negative that's for sure.'

She started whacking me. 'No problem like it was negative,' I went quick.

'No problem you're saying it was?'

'Tell you the truth Noreen,' I went confidential, 'only I never want to do that again.' Never did any harm letting birds clock a geezer's sensitive side now and then, made them get all cuddly. 'I got outside and I tell you I wondered about the future of the world and all them geezers not lucky like me to see it. I got so sad you might reckon it was me there was positive.'

'Oh Nicky,' she went stroking me although she did clock me a bit suspicious like I went over the top there. 'Oh Nicky, well you play your cards right and there won't never be any cause for another test will there?'

'Eh?' Jesus what territory was she staking out here?

'Well you know like I said, first off you stay out of trouble, then second you don't go round no other girls, well you know you might get to go steady with me, you hear what I'm saying?'

I was in deep here I was doing my pieces.

'No other birds Noreen?' Wrong thing to turn round and say, not what I meant to come out at all. 'Going steady Noreen?' Not heard anyone call it that in a long time. 'You mean sort of like permanent?'

'Take it one step at a time Nicky you don't need to be so eager, a girl's got to have time to think about the future.' Then she put her claws right up in my shirt making me shiver all over. 'You want me to stay tonight Nicky?' she went.

'Don't mind.'

So she whacked me again. Then she went 'Only I just got to go to the bathroom Nicky because these days I always wear a cap for making love you see.'

Which was where we got in the confusion.

So then after just a bit of explanation she sent me off up the bedroom while she got all set up taking her handbag in the bathroom.

Jesus.

I switched off the sounds and turned down the lighting and went in the bedroom and got in that bed. Nearly forgot to take my gear off I was that nervous, been a long time. Then she came in from the bathroom and she never wore any clothes, not even a cap. Least not on her bonce.

She was fucking gorgeous.

'Jesus Christ Noreen,' I went. She stood there a minute looking down on me. Then she got in the bed. She turned to me and just glued into me and she put her arms round me and we felt like we were very very friendly. It was brilliant.

★   ★   ★

Then my gob was in her hair and I was dribbling. She started to relax slow with little jerks time to time. She giggled and kissed me. Giggling made me come out of her and she went 'Ah'. I was grinning like an idiot and climbed off her and she went 'You got any tissues no I suppose not', and laughed. Then she turned over to me and hugged and clung to me and I went 'Yeah Noreen' and it still felt good even the time a geezer normally just wanted to roll over.

A bit later she went up the bathroom and

mopped up and brought some tissues back and told me to mop round the bed, it was my job. We kept giggling. Then she got in the bed again and snuggled up to me and went 'You're not thinking of sleeping yet are you Nicky? Men, I don't know. In the mood I am now Nicky, you got me worked up and I want to do it again soon, you know that?' Then she giggled again.

Jesus. Danger I could be collapsing again she went on like this. See she might be a trial to me that Noreen.

I hugged her. 'Feller got to get a bit of rest you know,' I went, and I cackled.

'Not too much then,' she went. She paused. Then she went 'That was beautiful Nicky.'

'Yeah,' I went. 'It was.'

# 15

Sunday morning eleven o'clock the phone rang. Noreen just went home. I was sitting there grinning like an idiot, not doing anything just sitting there spacey. I was knackered. I nearly lost count of how many times we did it (four). Then Noreen got in the shower, spruced herself up, did her eyes and went home looking like magic. Where she got the stamina I never knew, got to be special training.

Then the phone rang. It was that little Bridget off the paper. Good I wanted a talking with her, only a bit surprised she belled me Sunday morning. Bit surprised I gave her my number in the bargain, still no worries.

'Nicky I need to talk with you,' she went.

'Meet you in Jimmy's for breakfast?' I goes.

'That's fine. What time?'

'I got to cook lunch for an old lady. Half an hour. You pick me up here?'

'Fine.'

Then she rang back one minute later.

'I don't know where you live,' she turned round and said.

Told her, then got in the shower and she picked me up a few minutes later. In her little old 2CV for fuck's sake, fortunate none of my mates likely to be about that time of day or there was my rep gone for ever. We went up Jimmy's.

How we got there without her busting was something else. We got in and ordered tea and breakfast and she went 'Nicky I've got to tell you!'

'Yeah I knows.'

'You know? You know what I've got to tell you?'

'No, I only knows you got to tell me.'

'Oh. Well look. I've been going through the back copies of the *Guardian* over the last few days.'

'All them funerals and carnivals?'

'I've been going through looking to see if anything might have been hushed up. To see if anything about certain matters wasn't reported fully, maybe because influences went to work to stop us hearing. Like perhaps that post office you were involved in or the murder of DS Grant or the shooting up of your friend Jimmy's car.'

'Good idea like Bridget. Safe.' I was still knackered here and got a long day ahead, wanted a talk with her but never needed any extra grief in the ears. 'So what you find out

Bridget?' I went polite like.

'Well, nothing at all in that line I'm afraid.'

'Oh.' Bit of a downer that only still she hardly held herself from busting. So why was she giving it the promo? Never could be more than nineteen that Bridget only now she clocked like thirteen.

'But guess what?' she went.

'Can't guess.'

'I found out that throughout the last two or three years certain people, like you understand certain people, have been seen together more often than you might imagine.'

Ah.

Now we were talking.

'Carry on,' I goes.

'At receptions, at Council meetings, at weddings, funerals, at the dog track, at openings of new buildings, launches of job programmes, promotions of new car models, neighbourhood watch schemes, AGMs of housing associations, oh, you name it.'

She already did.

'Carry on,' I goes.

'Well, obviously in any town some people are going to know each other and turn up at the same functions. But here there's a certain collection together far more often than you might ever think natural. Not all of them all the time but some of them all the time or almost.' She got so excited she leaned over her tea and I never could help it only I had to clock down her T-shirt and register half her tits. Never mind though, back to business. 'And one of them' — she shifted round to be sure no-one was earwigging — 'one of them is our editor, Tiar Maginnes.'

'Tiar? Kind of a name's Tiar?' I never heard of him.

'No, T. R., like initials. Calls himself T.R. First name's Thomas, no-one knows the second, we call him Rasputin. Anyway, he likes to have his finger in everything, wants to be the power in the borough which is one reason we call him Rasputin. He's about thirty, looks about twenty and thinks he's going to be editor of the *Daily Mail* when he's forty. He gets in everywhere in the paper. And I couldn't help seeing he's always about with all the people we were talking about, he's got his picture taken with one of them or someone like them almost every week!'

'Huh.' Maybe she got something here. Put the control on the news, especially who had to be behind bits of work.

'Maybe you got something here Bridget,' I went.

'I have.'

They brought our breakfast. Least they brought my breakfast, she got Ryvita and jam, fuck knows where they found the Ryvita in Jimmy's. We chewed on our nosh and we gave it all a bit of thought.

'Bridget,' I went, 'girl, now you considered how happy this Tiar going to be when he finds out you're investigating him?'

'Um,' she went. 'So what you're saying is he might not be very happy is that right? I suppose, um, you might have a point there Nicky.'

'Might have a point there Bridget mate. Maybe you got to watch out for yourself a bit you know. Possible your editor might not be very happy. Fact he could get upset. Then he gets upset he might get an attitude. A real attitude.'

'You think my job could be at risk?'

I nearly blew my tea out my hooter. 'Yeah well I was never thinking so much on your Uncle Bob,' I goes, 'I was thinking more on the lines of you might get hold of some serious grief here.'

'Oh I see. Things could get nasty.'

No need for taking that one much further. I made progress on the breakfast and she nibbled on her Ryvita. Looked fatter already. 'Only just take care when you write out that list,' I goes.

'List?'

'Like a list. You heard how we reckon

there's that conspiracy round the borough. Now you started to suss it, find a few links. So you better make a list eh, names and dates and pictures and that, gather the evidence innit?'

'Well yes, I did start something like that at work, perhaps I should keep it somewhere else safe, do you think?'

'Good for you girl. Safe.'

Only there was still one other little problem I wanted to put out an airing round her way.

'Like there was something else I been meaning to ask you about them lists you're making up,' I goes.

'Yes Nicky?'

'Like, when you make up them lists you got to be putting names in the frame you understand? And them names in them frames got to be some of the time about bits of work innit?'

'Well, yes, that's the point of it, isn't it?'

'Exactly, yeah . . . yeah of course. Only you see mate, when all this gets noisy we got to ask you . . . you got to be going a bit light on one or two, er, petty offenders like hardly even guilty innocent parties you get my meaning?'

'Like who?'

'Like me mates Jimmy and Dean and them. You got to appreciate see, them things them big geezers never wanted them little geezers doing, well them things weren't all exactly totally over the board strictly legit eh?'

'You mean they were crimes? That's fairly obvious Nicky isn't it?'

'Well . . . put it like that you could call it that, yeah crimes I reckon.' I giggled. 'Things a geezer gets put up the Magistrates for now and again, maybe not even guilty of, know what I mean?'

'Yes Nicky I think I do. So what you're saying is, you want me to suppress news of the crimes your mates commit, just because this syndicate of bigger criminals was stepping on their turf and taking their crimes, is that about the size of it?'

All sudden I was never in charge of this interview.

'Well yeah,' I turned round and went.

She cackled. 'See what we can do Nicky,' she went tapping her little mitt on mine. 'See what we can do. Now about this list . . . '

Not quite the way I got it all planned, still we got there in the end working on that list of hers. She got connections all over the shop was going to make it a lot easier when it panned out. And she already took a few copies, showed them there and then in Jimmy's. 'Shit thanks mate,' I went. 'We got a result here. Now you put these somewhere safe you hear and you stay out and take care you hear? You hear what I'm saying?'

'I hear what you're saying.'

★   ★   ★

I got an answer machine fitted on my dog and bone before I went up Jamaica. Never wanted one on the mobile too expensive, only in the flat. Now we arranged all our parties kept in touch with me through the week while I kept low. So Sunday when I got back from the afternoon eating and yacking with Mrs Shillingford came a stern message from that Paulette.

'Nicky I shall ring you again at eight o'clock tonight,' she turned round and said. 'Be there.' Jesus I was having some agg with women telling me the score. 'And,' she added, 'don't leave no fucking message just be there.'

She rang at eight o'clock. 'This is a recorded message for Paulette,' I went. 'I'm busy right now taking a massage with Naomi Campbell can I call you back later?'

'Piss off Nicky,' she went, 'you at home now?'

'Course I'm at home now I'm talking to you innit?'

'You be there in fifteen minutes? Right, me

and Elvis is coming round.'

Put it down and the phone rang again. It was Rameez. 'Nicky you there?' he went. 'I'm cruising man, look you up now, you right? Be there fifteen minutes.' I never spoke even went hello so he mouthed it like he got the answer machine. Come round anyway, maybe he reckoned I was out so he could have a night drinking with the answer machine.

Then fuck me there was a knock on the door and it was George.

'Nicky this is most irregular,' he went while he came up the stairs. 'Can't think how I got involved in this, don't remember I ever agreed to it even. Here I am consorting with thieves and villains after hours, then during working hours instead of feeling a few collars there I am following a senior probation officer! How did I ever get into this?'

'What you want, George, rum or cannabis?' I went.

'And my missis is wondering what's happening with me being out after teatime. I took on doing warrants in the first place so I was home for tea, none of that shift rubbish.'

'She think you got a fancywoman George or what?'

'Dunno what she thinks. I'll just have a cup of tea please Nicky, and I'll thank you not to bring the drugs out until after I've gone.'

'Don't want me to slip none in your rosie?'

'No thank you I can do without being uninhibited and out of control. A little bit too old for all that.' There was a knock on the door. 'Who in hell's that then?' No-one called round George's unless they booked an appointment annually.

'Either Rameez or that Paulette George, both due for a reporting.'

'Dear oh law, more villains. Not that Paulette mind she's a little darling, running for England these days ain't she?'

'And making plenty of wedge George.' I got the door and it was the three of them all turned up together, Paulette and Elvis and Rameez. 'Well well,' I went letting them in, 'George here just turned round and said he was never wanting to meet all them villains here like Paulette and Elvis and Rameez, then would you believe it you all walked in.'

'Paulette I never!' went George. 'I was only just saying how you were a little darling one of the best. And you too Elvis, far as I know you're clean as a whistle.'

'Just leaves you Rameez,' I went.

Rameez cackled. Be an insult anyone called him clean.

'Evening Mr Marshall,' went Paulette. 'All right George?' went that Elvis.

'And George reckons I got to keep them

drugs hid up till he's away,' I went. 'Later we shoot up that opium, till then you all get cups of tea, right? Oh and that rum I brought back from Jamaica nearly forgot, unless you start injecting it that is.'

I made the kettle, still proud as a fart about my gaff and the kettle and I got four mugs so I drank my tea out of a glass. Brought it all in the living room and we sat about.

'Thank you Nicky,' goes George.

'Very nice tea Nicky,' goes Paulette.

'Where that rum?' goes Elvis. 'Hey, that just the sort my dad drink man, Wray and Nephew.'

'Well, what you got?' I went.

Then they all started talking at once.

Never stopped. All yacked over the top each other. They never went 'excuse me' or 'after you' or 'shut the fuck up' like you were supposed to. They all gabbed all the time. Year previous and Rameez would have sliced anyone yacked over him. Got to be he mellowed.

'Shut the fuck up!' I went.

So they did.

'Now what you got?' I went. 'Want it in good order geezers, where you been, who you clocked, who they get a meeting with, the monte. Paulette you make the list sister, birds write better innit?'

'Comes of being more intelligent Nicky. Only how come it's always sister this and sister that when you want something, you noticed that?'

'No I never noticed that and fuck knows how come it's this and that and how's your father, just do the fucking writing Paulette eh?' She cackled, we were always good mates me and Paulette except she was always bigger and faster than me. So she got a felt tip and big bits of paper, matter of fact she brought them with her so maybe she anticipated. Then she wrote the list.

It went:

1. Armitage.
2. Cousins.
3. Higgs.

Then she wrote:

1. Rameez and Co.
2. Me and Elvis.
3. Mr George.

'You taking the rise Paulette?' went George.

Then she turned round and said: 'Take it away Rameez. Give us the story man.'

So Rameez started.

'Well there we was like,' he went. He stopped a bit. Then he took a big breath and he closed his eyes and he was away like he was living it out for real again until he stopped.

'Well there we was like!' he went. 'There we was outside Chingford nick eight o'clock Tuesday morning like I'm sitting here innit! Only nothing happened Tuesday. He came to work — he went home. Case you ever want to feel his missis, he lives 24 Ravenscourt Rd, Cheshunt. We followed him there.'

'Er, hrmph,' went George, not very comfortable.

No putting off Rameez now though. 'So then we went back up Cheshunt early Wednesday, stayed up all night clubbing matter of fact, got to that home of his six o'clock a.m. in the morning. Followed him in, like pursuit. And you believe where he went? Only Mickey Cousins's yard? He got there seven o'clock a.m. and had a right chatting with that Mickey, and we got them both on our camcorder. Then he went to work. Then again that evening he never went home until later, he went up the Alfred Hitchcock, no less a place, and he had a little drink-up with two geezers who we also got on that camcorder, one the manager of that big Sainsbury's, other works up the

Council. Check it out.'

'Hey,' we all went.

'Then Thursday you listen up to this he went up the dog track! He went up that dog track and you know what happened there?'

'Tell it Rameez,' goes Elvis.

'He met fifteen people up some dinner bar up the Ascot Suite and two of them were Mickey Cousins and that Annabel Higgs and two more were them geezers he met up the Hitchcock and one was that mayor woman you know? And them all we got on that video too!'

'Hey! Rameez! Fine work man!'

He beamed. Least he beamed far as all his injuries let him. He was happy. He sipped his rum.

'Right George,' we all went. 'You next man.'

'Well, this is all most irregular,' he went.

We all cackled.

'All right, I may have mentioned that before. Well, it's very strange how this seems to be leading up to the same conclusion. Or maybe it's not strange, seeing what we know.

'This lady has a lot of meetings, hard to tell what they're all for. Goes up the Town Hall, all sorts. But I can tell you' — he consulted his notebook like they do in court, nearly asked permission off the judge — 'she had meetings over four days with the Director of Housing and the Head of Social Services and the mayor, Mary Lenton.'

'The mayor?'

'And she had lunch with Parvez Khan the Council leader and then a Greek dinner with Alfie Burman the big roofer and that geezer who's editor of the paper. And then — she went down the dog track on Thursday!'

'Yeah!'

'In the Ascot Suite like you know. Outside which I saw Rameez and Javed and the rest taking their little Polaroids.' He smirked.

Rameez was gutted. 'Hey, we was very discreet, we like blended in the background. How you spotted us, George?'

George snorted. 'You forget I am a trained police officer.' We all snorted. 'And you being the only Asians in the whole of the crowd may have helped.'

'You done good George,' I went. 'You done good.'

He was gratified.

We sipped on our tea.

So next I turned round to that Paulette and Elvis. 'What you got on the news then, you two?' I asked. 'What you seen on Mickey Cousins? You still did all that training all week Paulette?'

'Yeah course. Only that Elvis was a hero,

sometimes he had to go out following on his own. Innit Elvis?'

Elvis smoothed his locks down and grinned, modest. 'Only trouble was,' he went, 'I kept getting all this hero bit only that Paulette still never would go up no club with me. I never got this trouble before. You understand my position Nicky, beautiful fit bird like Paulette, you sit there all week paying attention to her muscles and she still won't never go out clubbing with you one night?'

'Jesus got to be hard Elvis, and you such a hero an' all. You never took pity on him Paulette, and him such a fucking sharp geezer in the bargain?'

'Hey,' went George. 'Hang about a minute you lot, we're trying to conduct an operation here, remember? What's the results on Mickey Cousins then, eh?'

'Oh yeah nearly forgot,' went Elvis. He braced up again. 'So we tell you what we got then. First off we got Mickey at his yard Tuesday seven in the morning when that Armitage came. And course we also got Rameez and Aftab and Afzal on our own camcorder while they were videoing them others. Very nice pics Rameez.'

'Shit!' went Rameez. We fell about.

'Then we got that editor you told about,

came with some geezer in a sponsored motor we reckon's from the Orient. Then Wednesday night we went up Commercial Road down the east. Followed him up there in my motor.'

'Luminous BMW,' went Paulette. 'Three-tone motor, Black Man's Wheels with a pink stripe down the side. Not quite Linford's class, eh? Down there in gangster land. Mickey meeting his mates down them high class Chinese places. We never stopped I'm telling you, we were right out of there.'

'Me, I'd have took them,' went Elvis, 'no problem, only Paulette she got a bad case of chicken and chips.'

'Elvis you was shitting yourself so hard I could hear bricks dropping,' goes Paulette. 'We was out of there.'

'Reckon Mickey goes back up his old manor sometimes,' George went. 'He comes from up east in the old days. Sees his mates maybe. Well-known meeting places those restaurants.'

'You reckon it's regular?' I goes. 'You reckon maybe he fixes up the labour there? Get the hired help in for bits of work up our borough?'

'Now you're talking. We get TT in and he could find out. Mind you I wouldn't fancy asking questions up the Chinese about their best customers, still the local CID might have an eye on it. It must be we could find out.'

'Then,' Elvis carried on, 'Thursday night Mickey went up the dog track.'

'Yeah!'

'With them others. And we got Rameez on that camcorder again.'

'Shit,' went Rameez. George cackled.

'And you too Mr Marshall,' went Paulette. 'We got some nice pics of you if your wife wants some.'

'No!'

We all howled.

★   ★   ★

We had some more of that rum. Forgot about the tea.

'So what we got?' I turned round and said.

'I'll tell you what we got,' went George. 'We got a police situation here, a major police situation which we get out of like straight away. This is the big league. There'll have to be enquiries off the Chinese, means police, be tricky. Enquiries off the dog track. Be no trouble, they'll co-operate, no reason not to. We've got to find out if they always got a dinner meeting Thursdays. If they do then that's maybe a good place to start. But this is very deep water, we're talking about the Chief

Super being elastic, and I tell you that means the Commissioner or even higher. Oh my God. So we've got to go official and we've got to do it tonight. We get TT tonight and if we don't get him I go straight up the Yard, Jesus I don't even know where it is. And we forget about us lot. We cancel tomorrow's meeting at Whipps Cross. You lot all done well, in fact you've been ace, I can't fault you. Now we go official from this moment on.'

Fair enough George, I reckoned. 'Fair enough George,' we all went. None of us meant it of course. He'd be getting TT on his mobile now, TT cut it off when he gave me his card only George had it. Nice surprise for TT late on Sunday night when he got the call, all of us pissed as rats.

Never occurred to George I might still have one or two plans he never needed to know about. Funny thing I found hard to forget geezers trying to snuff me in Jamaica. Let the pigs take over maybe, and maybe even get a bit of protection off them. Only you got your face to think about and they surely dissed me. Got to be I put in an appearance.

Reckoned some of my mates could want on putting in an appearance in the bargain, feel they got a few sore points to clear up. Needed the odds right like ten to one our way, then maybe the right time to put a few words in.

Then again there was what they did to Noreen.

★ ★ ★

In case I had any doubt it, next off something nasty went down. Something very nasty and I reckoned very bad manners.

There we were all sipping and swilling and feeling mellow and nice, and George starting to make it on the phone calls. Then out of nothing came the biggest whoosh and roar you ever heard, and right outside my gaff.

'Fuck me!' goes Rameez first.

'Fuck me!' goes the rest of us. The windows shook and rattled but they stayed. Whatever it was it was outside still. Downstairs though not so lucky, hear the crashing and tinkling. We fell flat on the floor, stayed there till it all went quiet then still stayed clear of the windows. It started howling downstairs. Hear people collecting outside. We went down the stairs and out slowly. Nothing there except some glass, although most of it blew in the flat below. And blue flame.

Any fucker can make a petrol bomb. Milk bottle fill up with petrol, put a bit of rag in, light it and throw it. Whoosh.

You got to be able to throw straight though

279

you want to get it in a window. Before the big bang there was a smaller crash. They aimed up my window only they hit the wall, it fell back then it blew out the downstairs windows. The neighbours never sat there expecting a petrol bomb, didn't take it very calmly.

'Fuck me,' I went while Old Bill started turning up. I was shaking like a fucking leaf.

'They followed one of us or they were after you Nicky or they wanted us all together,' goes Rameez. Rameez's bottle long since gone after the last business. Me I never had any bottle to lose.

'Just let me get on that phone again,' George turned round and went soft after he had a few verbals with the plod squad. 'We got to get going here very quick but very quiet. Only first I'm going to get someone to watch this place the next few days. Don't suppose they'll come back but no harm in being sure. Jesus my missis'll kill me being out this late.'

'No problem George. You do what you got to do mate.'

And I was even surer now what I got to do. I got to get after that Armitage was The Voice. But first I reckoned I recognised the style, and first I was making my way round Mickey Cousins.

# 16

Fact was I never had a lot to do the next couple of days. Lot of time spent belling everyone for setting up some little plans, cancelling a few other arrangements. Never used the same phone twice. Then looked for some bits keeping myself busy. Went down the gym up Kelmscott a couple times on my UB40 cheap rate, put back some of the muscle I lost since I came away from the prison gym. Keep up the physio on my injuries in the bargain. Went round visiting Mum, took her the Gangsta T-shirt I brought her from Jamaica. Poked Noreen a couple more times on the Tuesday. No, three more times. All observed, in a manner of speaking, by the police protection George fixed up down the corner of the street. Then I went round retailing coffee.

They loved it that coffee. Took some round the Caribbean restaurants the rest down Soho. Coffee specialists and delis it was like they sudden started mainlining when they sniffed those little beans. Still loose in the bag never got Blue Mountain written on it, still they sniffed it and ground a little then snorted it again then they smiled wide and it was like instant dosh they smelled frying in the pan. Smelled all the same to me like any coffee, only straight away they slapped it in a jar and charged four times over, no danger.

So we were making plenty of paper.

Then I sat in my gaff getting used to being domestic. Took the sheets down the launderette again after Noreen visited, have to get another set. Made some meals and clocked videos and drank a bit of rum. No-one to fuss you, make a cup of tea when you want and just have to hope no fucker chucks a petrol bomb in to warm the place up. So I sat there being domestic and I was getting ready for an appointment on Wednesday night. I made some arrangements for that day and I wanted to be in a good frame of mind. Chilled.

Then Wednesday night I put on my best gear and went up Chingford for paying my respects up Mickey Cousins. Right up north Chingford where his gaff was you had to put on your best gear.

I took Rameez with me and Aftab and Afzal. And Dean Longmore and Jimmy Foley. We reckoned Wednesday was a good night for visiting him, so Thursday when they all got together up the dog track they got something for yacking about while they sipped their cocktails. Something for yacking about meant something for Old Bill listening up. We always did want to help the police with their enquiries.

Then again there was one other good reason for visiting by Mickey. Most of us owed Mickey one and never wanted to miss the opportunity for giving him our best wishes. After Thursday he might be out of circulation. Be a right shame we missed out on paying him a social one up north Chingford.

This was it. We were making our moves.

★ ★ ★

Everyone knew where Mickey Cousins lived, I grew up knowing where Mickey Cousins lived. His business was off The Mount, his home was up by the forest looking out over the fucking golf course.

We took him at home.

We had two choices Wednesday. Wednesday nights we knew now he went down Commerical Rd for chatting his mates and setting up some villainy. So we could take him there in among the Mercs and Daimlers parked outside the Chinese. Or we could take him at home.

While we still fancied breathing it was best we took him at home.

Commercial Rd you never walked right and paid your respects you were dead meat. Got to be stomach out head back and walk very wide. Then you got to know who were the guvnors and look very straight at them before you went out shooting whoever they told you. Look crooked and they hung you off a meat hook.

North Chingford you were safer. Granted we were still off our patch only you knew the neighbours were never gangsters. Builders or city types or dentists only never gangsters. Trespass on the golf course and maybe a dentist came after you tried to give you an extra filling only never a gangster with a shooter.

We never had to tail Mickey. Whenever he went out he dropped his minder off in Highams Park then came on home. Always the same, never expected any rubbish and never got it. No need to get your knickers twisted. On the other hand run the business that way and you get kind of cocky, kind of careless.

Which was what we were counting on. Shitting ourselves all the same but counting on him getting careless.

We took three motors, family motors we borrowed off families on Waltham Way. I never lifted any of them personal, had to stay clean for that Noreen or I never got her in bed any more. Hoped she never minded Allowing To Be Carried, petty offence. We watched for Mickey from round the corner not on his street. We waited outside the takeaway on Station Rd.

We waited half an hour then he came.

From Highams Park where he dropped the minder he always came up Kings Rd then Station Rd. We picked him up coming up Station Rd from behind where we were parked, no mistaking his lights. He turned up his street nice and easy. We gave him one minute for getting indoors.

Careful preparation and we could maybe clock his moves every Wednesday when he got home, like how long he was downstairs and did he get his fucking cocoa before he went up and did his missis wait up for him and give it him on the settee. Only we never had time for careful preparation. Earlier we did spot his missis put the lights out downstairs and that was it.

Mickey was on his second missis as it happened, traded the first in for a younger model. Bit later he got a couple of kids by her. Kids were somewhere in his gaff got to be.

So after one minute we went round the corner in his street and parked up outside his place. Never locked the doors on the motors.

Mickey did keep his hutch nicely locked up though. There were plenty bolts and chains all over the doors and the alarm there just for letting you know.

Only we never planned on using the doors, and fuck the alarm we weren't thinking on staying around for a quick coffee with the Bill before bedtime.

Aftab and Afzal went round the back. Rameez and me in the front. Dean and Jimmy in reserve or looking out the neighbourhood watch or fucking whatever. Case the Bill drove past, Dean and Jimmy showed themselves then did a runner draw them away.

We gave Aftab and Afzal thirty seconds getting over the fence up to the house. Then we went in the garden up the front window. First crash came when they put the back window in. We put the window in round the front for the next crash. Double glazing so it took twice as long. We were equipped though, put the bats in. We stepped through Mickey's window barely a scratch and there he was coming out the toilet very hasty. Wondering what all the noise was.

'Evening Mickey,' I went. Then I whacked him with the bat.

There he was nice and dozy after his grub

and a few bottles of the old vino. Get home and take a quiet piss and what do you find but four lads come in to give you a whacking.

We already decided no blades though unless it got necessary.

Aftab gave him the first kick. Got him in the solar. As he staggered Afzal hit him up the hooter. From his spurting I got blood on my best gear.

Mickey was backed against the toilet door now. Rameez hit him with a rice flail maybe cracked a rib or two. Afzal punched him in the throat made him gag and dribble. I whacked him in the gut then we all did, made him throw up while he was gagging meantime. Pity to spend all that wedge down the Chinese then have it come back on you all over your carpets.

He went down and we gave him a good kicking. We kept it controlled though even Rameez. We never wanted him brown bread, we never wanted any loss of memory or even unconscious. We wanted him hurting and hurting bad, and we wanted everyone to know.

Whole thing took maybe twenty seconds.

Already it started to get very noisy, what with the sounds of the whacking and then the alarm ringing and his missis going 'Mickey! Mickey! Is that you what's happening?' very loud from upstairs. Mickey was very quiet you had to say, just went down lovely and peaceful.

We were gone.

Walked out the front door down the path out the gate and got in the motors. Set out in three different directions, none of them Station Rd where the Bill had to come down. We all heard the sirens just after we set off, quite likely his alarm was connected up the copshop. Only I was away in one motor down Woodford, not bad motor Audi as it goes. Dean and Jimmy were round the back streets and the others took off down Highams Park. We were confident on the Old Bill getting no news from Mickey about who we were paid him a visit.

I crossed the North Circular and ditched the motor round Whipps Cross, shit I reckoned I committed an offence after all driving a stolen motor. Still too late now, put it down to inexperience and bad planning. I legged it round the back of Wood St up Shernhall then Church Hill Rd till I got to my place.

We never left any message back there. We reckoned Mickey got the message. Now we waited to see what brought them out Thursday, whether they heard about the message too.

I checked for seeing how my guards were outside my gaff. Only they never were. Maybe they got the sudden call up Chingford or maybe they went off for a drink-up and a massage, either way they were never guarding me now. Bit of a result maybe, never witness my time of arrival. I got in my door.

Then I sat up there and shook. Sat and shook and gaped up the ceiling. This was never my game. I was too old. I never had the bottle. I never wanted to die. I sat and shook half the night then lay down and had nightmares.

Consolation was though Mickey probably got his troubles too.

# 17

There was Old Bill all over the shop.

Two o'clock in the afternoon it was like a fucking film studio. On the street there was nothing to show. No uniforms no Pandas, nothing for giving out a warning. Everyone drove in quiet and separate like they came to feed the dogs or clean the toilets. Put the motors away. Then inside the building was like Wembley before Madonna went on stage.

Geezers in T-shirts and jeans lying in corners with screwdrivers. Technicals in white coats and paintbrushes laying the dust for the prints then sort out a bit of DNA on the side, mop up a bit of spit and howsyourfather then reckon it matched your granddad and maybe Jack the Ripper. Tall birds in specs drinking tea out of flasks taking snaps of empty rooms, fuck knows why keep 'em happy. Very important gaffers in suits and hats from up the Yard stood about grunting. Special investigation unit always popular with the plods, only this time make it even more popular they got real guvnors in the bargain.

All quiet except for the grunting. Seemed

like you never turned round and spoke after you got up the Yard. Never went out for a piss-up and Tandoori Saturdays like most Old Bill either, all you did was grunt and eat Kit-Kats. It was the biz.

TT was like a pig in shit. He was so happy he wanted to roll about in it only the same time he was so nervous he reckoned he picked his hooter and they terminated him. These were the geezers on the big expenses. These were the geezers got asked to join the Masons and go up Malaga with villains. Geezers got a driver for their motors and read the *Times* plonked on the leather in the back. Heavy duty geezers. Wore brown shoes.

Then they got the hit men. Thin pale geezers laying around outside on the roofs wearing camouflage and tracksuits. Maybe reckoned it was a jungle up Walthamstow. They brought their sandwiches and coffee and little briefcases. Seemed like they knew something I never, expected the mayor to shoot her way out.

It was busy.

All started Monday morning. TT never knew where to head for so he went for what he knew, tried the CID Inspector out of Chingford and hoped he never bent with the big man. Turned out a fluke, the pig was a straight one, name of Farrow. You never clocked him for dust while he was going up the Yard.

Then they came down and they talked to TT and they talked to George and that Karen Mohammed, in the bargain they even came round my way with a big sniff. Nice to co-operate with the guardians of the law. They hauled TT and George and that Karen up London where they did a lot of listening some place with bare walls and George reckoned no tea machine. They came round my place and I entertained them at home. Made a change them ringing the bell, I was only used to the law kicking the door in. Pity really. They kicked the door in and you got a call later off the inspector offering the dosh for a new one. Always reckoned they booted the door in so you never got time for flushing the drugs away, only a lot more likely they just liked a good booting. Could have done with a new door.

So I entertained them at home and they asked a lot of questions polite like. Then I entertained Jimmy and Dean and Rameez and Elvis and Paulette and Sharon and they asked them a lot of questions polite like too. Members of the public we were. Even time to time it looked like the reason we met up with these villains was maybe we crossed the traffic wardens or never got a bus ticket or one or two other things, they still never got technical with us. Never promised immunity either mind, still never got fussy.

Then George reckoned they got a few ministers in. Meantime they made the plans for the dog track Thursday how we told them in the first place.

George took a look in the stadium before he went home for his tea. Never mind what the fuck was going down, George got to be home for his tea or there were ructions.

Natural they never wanted us in. Their big secret never wanted the scum in. Only thing was I slipped in eleven o'clock when the place was like a morgue. Two o'clock it was Wembley stadium and they never kicked me out. TT had a word, they grunted a fair bit only never kicked me out.

First they kept a few people away from the area till later. Armitage got a message sudden planning meeting up London. Tiar Maginnes got called away to his board.

Annabel Higgs was up her HQ somewhere and they sorted a couple of others the same. Mickey I heard was up Whipps Cross getting a spot of intensive care. In pain I hoped. Most of the rest the Old Bill had to hope for the best. Only keep it dead stum round the stadium.

Management of the track co-operated no

problem. No reason they had not to, specially two dozen very heavy Old Bill told them. Ran a nice clean shop up the stadium, family entertainment and borrow all your family dosh. All they knew about happenings Thursdays was some geezer booked the Ascot Suite for a regular crowd. None of their business what for, leading heads of the borough and made with the Visa cards.

Ascot Suite came in at minimum twenty-five gobs for dinner at £25 a throw, so you were talking folding money here. Only got ten gobs you still paid for twenty-five. Turned out they normally got about fifteen. Met in good time, got their dinner then the waitresses cleared out and they had a little natter while the dogs started. Little natter stitching up the borough's crime the next week or so. Then near the end they clocked the dogs maybe had a couple bets.

And today Old Bill was there waiting for them.

They never wanted us around like I said only they never fussed. My mates were coming later with the punters in case the pigs wanted any assist here. After all we got an interest, fuckers were taking our living away. Got an interest clocking justice being done here.

After that Sunday when we finished our surveillance Old Bill started their surveillance, and the manor went quiet like the fucking Mafia just hit town. No question doing any work. Start a spot of Supply and half Scotland Yard got you on camera. Go on a bit of Interfering and it was like Blackpool Illuminations the flashes going off. You never ever spotted so many BT engineers and dustmen and roadworkers standing about in one town not doing a lot. Pity they all got big feet and looked like PE instructors. Even the fucking parking Hitlers got doubled, twice as many complaints as ever in the *Guardian* on the fucking privatised fines now. All very discreet.

But they built the links round the borough heads. Made a pretty picture so we heard later, got them stitched right up.

Once you sussed the game it never took a lot of imagination, even the Bill sorted it out. Mickey supplied the labour like I said, Thursdays they planned the bits of work, put the work and the labour together. Post offices, warehouses, protection, supply, massage, housing divvies, motors, even tow-aways. Anything got big enough spends they controlled it, kept it in the family, in the borough. Did the books nice, shared it up. Fucking creamed it.

Oh and they did a little bit of learning where they needed to. Never bothered you were lifting a Mars Bar out of Woolworths, only you stepped across their territory and they put a bit of influence down. One step and they put it down to a misunderstanding, you got a verbal. Two steps and they whacked you heavy.

DS fucking Grant knew too much and they wrote the ending.

And no-one grassed them up. Not in anyone's interest getting hurt. So the borough was under control.

Until now.

The Yard reckoned they were bound to get it all sorted by Thursday. Do the watching, do the linking then get in place and do the listening. Only just in case they needed a kick-start we gave them an assist on Wednesday up Mickey's, give him a little dusting. Just for putting a bit of word round, just to get the conversation going like.

Might reckon it was all part of crime prevention, maybe give us a fucking award. Help the Old Bill bring law and order back to the borough so you could go out nick a motor in peace like the old days. Except me, of course I gave up crimes on account of that Noreen.

Late afternoon I went home and got a

shower and cup of tea up my gaff. Guards were back there again today. I went in and lay on the bed a few minutes giving it the thinking. Planning for what was going down. Was I nervous? Was I fuck, I was shitting myself.

I got a piece of toast then I toddled back up the dog track from my place in time for the evening's entertainment.

Down Hoe St to the Bell, up Chingford Rd and over the Billet. I took it slow. From a distance the stadium was lit up, bring the punters off the North Circular maybe going 'Whoo whassat?' then get drawn in like moths. Charlie Chan's got its lights on too already for the ravers. Minibuses and motors were starting filling up the car parks over the street, folk playing in the traffic getting across the road. Essex people maybe not used to traffic. Everyone mellow no hurry. Racing starting some time soon so get in casual. I wandered in slow.

One other reason I wandered in slow was on account of I got something stashed down my trouser leg might come in useful later. Little souvenir I brought back out of Jamaica, exchanged it up country for a pair of trainers. Nice and shiny it was, long and curling slightly. Machete. Kept it in a piece of cloth. Some reason it never caused agg on the metal detector up customs. Reckoned it was a pen knife maybe.

Still in the piece of cloth or it could scratch. Only you had to walk slow all the same. Brought it along just in case, never know when you wanted to cut down a few plantains or green bananas.

Paid my dosh on the gate and got a programme then slid in the main stand quiet. Reckoned best to start off up the Stowaway Lounge sort of ooze in gradual. So up the escalator and mingle with the punters.

I never knew where they found their punters. Not regular birds and geezers out of Walthamstow or even Chingford, know what I mean. All the birds blonde. Geezers weighty. Few Turks no Asians no blacks. Everyone gobbing their three-course nosh very mellow and getting nicely pissed up. Filled out their betting slips and waddled up the tote. Not good preparation for most things I knew getting all that grub in them, still maybe they never expected most things I knew. Everyone betting now. A few studying form. Waste of time I heard studying form on account of when they wanted to fix it they gave the dogs a dose of Largactyl in with their bowl of Chum. Stop them coming first, stop them getting schizophrenic clocking God over their left shoulder in the bargain. Very handy.

Most the punters though too pissed by now for studying form or anything else much, probably betting on their street numbers like as not.

Sounds coming out the speakers ever so gentle. Grannie music Buddy Holly and Neil Sedaka. Punters all ages only never seemed to mind the grannie music. Weird. Kept them nodding slowly while they handed over the housekeeping, nicker here nicker there, hardly even notice your pocket empty.

I got a coffee and went through the next bar. No hurry winkling my way down the Ascot Suite, Mickey's friends were probably spending the first half the evening yacking about him. I stood up a corner and clocked a race. Nearly as exciting as watching your beard grow.

Dog number three seemed like the fave round there. 'Go on three go on three go on three,' some blonde bit by me yelled. Seemed to reckon not only the dog heard through the glass it knew its number in the bargain. Only it came last so it probably got that Largactyl. The bird by me got droopy and went back to her Spumante.

I went outside. Half of Walthamstow and Chingford worked up the Stow somewhere. Half my school class behind the bar or waitressing going 'All right Nicky? You all right?' None of my school class selected for working with the cash on the tote, wonder why. I went outside in the air to keep a bit quiet and clock the action. TT was there probably some strategic spot.

He looked like he always did like fucking CID. Turned round and talked the same too. 'What the fuck you doing here?' he went. 'Thought you bleeding went home.'

I belled Sharon on the mobile. She was outside the gate, I kept Sharon out the way.

'Customer Comfort,' she went quick. She never knew any other intro now.

'What happen?'

'All going like the plan Nicky. They coming in. I seen three or four you showed me on the pics.'

'The fuck you doing?' goes TT.

'Only keeping a check TT, only keeping a check man. Make sure you Old Bill know how to handle a situation.'

'The fuck you want to keep out of this you little bleeder. This is proper police ops now doing it regular. We don't need you no more you got that?'

'Yeah yeah. Got that. Police ops were any fuckin' good they'd have nicked me a few more times. Best to have a back-up you ask me.'

Not a lot he could turn round and say to

that. Been in a fair pickle without us on this one in the bargain. Anyway his two-way kept bleeping now and he kept needing to call up Roger and Charlie. Things were warming. They were ready and fidgeting. They were about going in.

It was eight o'clock. Outside there was racing proper now, everyone involved plenty screaming and eating. No-one took any notice the Ascot Suite. Inside the Suite they were all in there and the doors shut. Sharon told me the ones she clocked outside. I spotted one or two faces and Dean and Jimmy were milling recognised a couple more. Even TT let on a bit. It was a big night in there tonight, and when they gobbed their grub up the waitresses came out left them with their booze to do their plenty talking.

Wired up by every technical in London. Wired out to copshops from Chingford down the Yard.

There was Armitage and Higgs and Tiar Maginnes. There was Parvez Khan the Council leader and Mary Lenton the mayor and Dawn Trujillo off Social Services. There was Kevin McWhirter out of Sainsbury's and Dave Kent off the Housing and Alfie Burman the builder. There was Derek Norris from the Orient and David Saunders manager of

Westminster Bank and Rev Stockwood from the Catholic. There was a pair of lawyers Donovan McClair and Terry Ainslie, top men up their firms, and Maureen Smithson head of education and Gary Down director of finance. There was Paul Manning chief clerk at the courts and Angela Fairey they reckoned was top magistrate. They got it stitched. There was eighteen there that night, maybe a few lucky ones got missing. One who definitely got missing was Mickey Cousins must have caught a bug.

I got along the outside a bit, get closer that way less interference. Never wanted to be missing the finale. Never ever wanted to give up my chances clocking Armitage going down. I mingled ever so easy with the punters outside, moved along then slipped round the back and found a door. It was open.

Went up some steps and along a passage. No-one was stopping you getting in on account of everyone was out the front now clocking the dogs. Or in the bars noshing. Except eighteen fuckers in the Ascot Suite and about a thousand Old Bill lying in corridors and under floors and up in the roofs listening up to them.

We heard after there was plenty of talking in there. TT told me later they got it in spades, enough to send them away in a convoy. News coming out their lugholes. News of motors news of supply news of robbings, news of plans all over. News of Mickey Cousins. Maybe they reckoned on sending him a few flowers although I doubted he was smelling much these days.

I slid along the passage. Then fuck me I nearly had a heart job. Wayne Sapsford was there. Never wanted to miss out did Wayne. Only trouble was Wayne got nicked every time he sneezed, nicked dropping a fag packet nicked thinking about a motor. Wayne lifted around a thousand motors in his time, got nicked on half of them. He was walking trouble, not the type of geezer you wanted around you in a crisis.

'Wayne what the fuck?' I whispered.

'Come to lend you my assist,' he goes.

'Better off my grannie,' I goes. 'She got a better record in punch-ups. You get arrested lifting some greyhound Wayne fuck everything up.'

'Shut up Nicky it all happening,' he goes. Not a lot I could turn round and say so we crept on.

Then they moved.

We just got to the Suite exit and met two geezers in suits and three geezers in flak jackets. Just in time to clock them going in. It was like my mum's front door when they booted it in. Pow.

Two main entrances they went in, and a couple of others they invented. Pow pow. Twenty thirty Old Bill in there all very fast, massive confrontation like a circus. Only a small room it was, just dandy for twenty-five diners and the staff squeezing by. Sudden it was filled up with eighteen diners and thirty Old Bill. Shouting. Room was full.

They were never messing. Same technique for robbery up a bank, fill the place with yelling shouting screaming bawling, frighten the fuck out of everyone. Not very likely they were loaded in there only no point messing. Bill went in fanning round the walls turning over tables facing up the fuckers. They were waving pointing kicking out so no-one on the fuckers noticed whether the law got shooters themselves. Fact was they got shooters only they kept them hid up among the specials. Now they stood there all of them like a victory.

Everyone the diners shut it like they were stuck. Looked like they got an electric shock. Gobs open glasses half way up. Then some of them cried out in their fear.

Then there was silence. Part of the plan too.

I slipped in just by the doorway.

Into that silence then came the speaker. Big man name of Miller, nice suit bad complexion. He stood up the middle and he shouted loud:

'NOW LISTEN UP ALL OF YOU! FIRST YOU ARTHUR JOHN ARMITAGE . . . '

He was about to start on the arrest and caution. Only he never got that far.

Armitage spotted me.

So it was all down to me? I was lurking in the corner minding my business. Fifty other folk in that room and he spotted me lurking quiet. The fucking way it went these days it looked like. And I wasn't ready for it. Or then again maybe I was.

'You! Burkett!' he cried out just like he did up Jamaica.

Then he was off.

Only a small room and he was across it. For a big fat geezer he moved quick.

All the fucking Old Bill in that room and he took them all startled. Tables already down so he was over the space. For extras he picked up a carving blade off the floor. Seemed for sure he reckoned this was it, he was already up shit creek so fuck it and go for the whole bundle. Or maybe he never reckoned anything at all, just got the fury in him and went for it.

Either way he was at me.

He got one uniformed kiddie looked like a fucking cadet hanging off him trying to hold him up. Armitage was too big for him, swatted him off and kept coming for his appointment. He got his hands out in front of him ready for my neck. One of them got the carver pointing in it.

I was frozen.

He was closer. Roaring.

Then I thought about that voice again and I remembered The Voice and I gave some thinking to that Noreen and her scar. And I gave some more thinking to the fear and the pain she got off that geezer.

Then I lifted that machete up and I tore his throat out.

★　★　★

One quick heavy slash from the side and that was it. Got him from the side of his neck round his jugular. So hard it jarred a nerve in my arm, quite a pity. Knocked him sideways while he stumbled staggered clutched his throat with both hands, one still got the carver looked like he did it himself. Weird painful noises coming out of him started with roaring and glugging then went glugging and roaring then just glugging.

Eyes staring all the while clocking me like the devil. Lasted four or five seconds, long seconds. Then he started falling. While he fell his blood came like a fountain spurting up the wall by the door frame. And he fell taking Wayne Sapsford with him fell on top of little Wayne like he was never there. Two three seconds more and there was gravy covered him all up poor little fucker Wayne.

And I stood there machete in my mitt. Fifty witnesses stood staring. Fifty fucking witnesses.

'It was an accident,' I turned round and said.

'Oh no,' I added.

Then I wished I never was born. I started the shaking. Not this all over again. I wanted my gaff I wanted that Noreen I wanted to walk down the High St and say all right to my mates. I never wanted to be killing chief superintendents. I never wanted killing anyone. I never wanted the custody I never wanted the nightmares I wanted a nice time. And I told Noreen I started going straight, no more nickings.

Had to admit it though he got it coming to him that Armitage. He got his deservings.

And I got fifty witnesses. No doubting I did it the one hand. No doubting self-defence on the other. Either way it was an accident got to be.

He lay there on top of Wayne and Wayne never moved, blood spreading all over him, shellshock. Then they got the first aid in then the ambulances, only it was just for show. Make no difference to Armitage how many ambulances they got. Then they started mopping up and arresting.

No more out of the suspects gave a murmur, hardly surprising case they reckoned I'd slice them. There was plenty mopping plenty arresting, all very quiet and peaceful.

Then they came to me. First off they put someone behind me stop me slipping out for a pint. Then they gave me a chair, then would you believe some police technical bird gave me a cup of tea out of her flask. Never spoke though none of them spoke to me yet.

First words they gave me were the arrest.

Maybe it was only precautionary I reckoned. Get police bail after I got Mrs Mellow my brief up there. Withdraw the charges.

After all I got fifty witnesses thirty of them Old Bill. Armitage got no witnesses. And anyone could clock it was an accident I hardly even knew what was happening.

Oh shit though. Here we went again.

We do hope that you have enjoyed reading
this large print book.

Did you know that all of our titles
are available for purchase?

We publish a wide range of high quality
large print books including:
**Romances, Mysteries, Classics**
**General Fiction**
**Non Fiction and Westerns**

Special interest titles available in
large print are:
**The Little Oxford Dictionary**
**Music Book**
**Song Book**
**Hymn Book**
**Service Book**

Also available from us courtesy of
Oxford University Press:
**Young Readers' Dictionary**
**(large print edition)**
**Young Readers' Thesaurus**
**(large print edition)**

For further information or a free
brochure, please contact us at:
**Ulverscroft Large Print Books Ltd.,**
**The Green, Bradgate Road, Anstey,**
**Leicester, LE7 7FU, England.**
**Tel:** (00 44) 0116 236 4325
**Fax:** (00 44) 0116 234 0205

*Other titles published by Ulverscroft:*

## VINNIE GOT BLOWN AWAY

### Jeremy Cameron

A Walthamstow native, nineteen-year-old Nicky Burkett has been in and out of trouble his whole life. When he finds the body of his best mate, Vinnie, at the bottom of a tower block minus his feet, Nicky's code of conduct dictates that he exact an appropriate revenge. The problem is, he's seriously outgunned — it would seem that Vinnie crossed some deadly criminals who have decided to take over the drug trade in the area. So Nicky sets out to persuade his allies and acquaintances to join his vendetta. But things don't go according to plan . . .

# THE RESCUER

## R. S. Hill

Bideford, 1873: The River Torridge is in flood. Almost as soon as she sets foot in the town, Abigail March saves a young woman from drowning. The daughter of a progressive Canadian politician, Abigail is here on official business, standing in for her father. Accompanied by Inspector Theodore Newton of the Metropolitan Police, she has travelled to Devonshire to inspect a captured shipment of firearms being guarded by the local police. That night, the woman she saved is murdered. Then the weapons are found to have disappeared. A man is arrested — but when Abigail befriends the brother of the accused, she and Newton believe a potentially tragic mistake has been made . . .

# ONE BULLET TOO MANY

## Paul Bennett

Life in the Polish resort on Lake Cezar is idyllic. That is, until local crime lord Emil Provda starts a protection racket among the local businesses. But this time, Provda has picked a fight with the wrong person. Hotel owner Stanislav is a former mercenary soldier — and when his former brothers in arms hear their old comrade is in trouble, they agree to come out of retirement for one final fight. Putting their lives on the line, Johnny Silver, Red, Pieter and Bull are determined to close Provda down if it's the last thing they do . . .